I Don't Remember the Steaks Until Quarter to Five.

I race downstairs, yank them out of the freezer, frozen together, wrap them in plastic, and run them under the hot-water tap. When they soften up a little I start prying them apart with a kitchen knife.

Then several things happen at once.

The knife slips.

My mother comes home.

The tip of the blade sails into my left wrist.

As she walks into the kitchen.

It's a deep cut; not much blood, but so sharp a blast of pain that I can't catch my breath or speak for a few seconds as I grasp the cut wrist with my other hand.

And she starts screaming. Her screams become my name ELIZABETH ELIZABETH.

I'm clutching my left wrist with my right hand and finally my voice comes back and I say IT WAS AN ACCIDENT KATHERINE IT WAS AN ACCIDENT I SWEAR IT WAS AN ACCIDENT.

It's going to be a long weekend.

"Elizabeth's ability to cope with disaster—with life itself—gradually grows, climaxing with a burst of understanding . . . an affecting, introspective novel."

—ALA *Booklist*

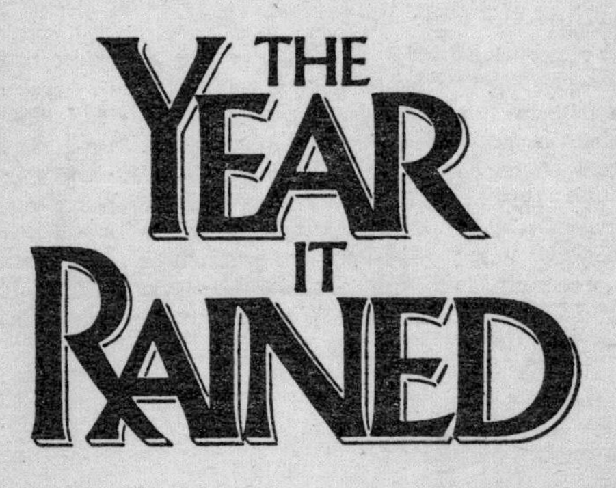

Crescent Dragonwagon

PUBLISHED BY POCKET BOOKS NEW YORK

This novel is a work of fiction. Names, characters, places and incidents are either the product of the author's imagination or are used fictitiously. Any resemblance to actual events or locales or persons, living or dead, is entirely coincidental.

Excerpts on pages 102 and 156 from "The Love Song of J. Alfred Prufrock" in *Collected Poems 1909–1962* by T. S. Eliot, copyright 1936 by Harcourt Brace Jovanovich, Inc., and Faber and Faber Limited; copyright © 1963, 1964 by T. S. Eliot. Reprinted by permission of the publishers. Excerpt on page 83 from *The Berlin Stories* by Christopher Isherwood, copyright 1935 by Christopher Isherwood. Copyright 1945, 1954 by New Directions Publishing Corporation. Reprinted by permission of the publisher. Excerpt on page 37 from the song "I Don't Worry 'Bout A Thing" by Mose J. Allison reprinted by permission of Audre Mae Music, BMI. Excerpt on pages 156-57 from "Southside Blues (monologue)" by Lou Rawls on the album *Lou Rawls Live* (SN-16097), copyright 1967 by Loulee Music, BMI. Reprinted by permission of the publisher.

POCKET BOOKS, a division of Simon & Schuster, Inc.
1230 Avenue of the Americas, New York, N.Y. 10020

Published by arrangement with Macmillan Publishing Co., Inc.
Library of Congress Catalog Card Number: 84-42980

For information address Macmillan Publishing Co., Inc.,
866 Third Avenue, New York, N.Y. 10022

ISBN: 0-671-62902-6

First Pocket Books printing January 1987

10 9 8 7 6 5 4 3 2 1

Printed in the U.S.A.

For my parents, now

e-piph-a-ny (i-pif′e-ne) n.
A sudden perception of the essential nature or meaning of something, as in a sudden flash of recognition. An intuitive grasp of reality through something (as an event) usually simple and striking.

Contents

THE
YEAR
IT
RAINED

One

In Transit

I HAVE the mother everyone wants.

It's a fact, just a fact. I am contemplating this simple fact on the Monday after the Sunday of my Uncle Jay's funeral. I am contemplating this simple fact as the train jerks and bounces its way into New York City, where I go to school and where my father now lives.

I am coming from Chilton, where I live with my mother, Katherine, and where, up until two months ago, my father, Walter, lived. My parents, whom I have called by their first names for as long as I can remember, are now separated. I think this time they really will divorce, something I have uneasily expected all my life.

There is no reason for me to like this train ride. The seats are stained, the floor is so gummy with stuff spilled in the past that sometimes my boots stick to it and make little clicking noises as I lift each foot, the windows are too smudged to get a good view of the dirty, beautiful Hudson River, which snakes alongside the railroad tracks. Often the train will just stop between stations, without any explanation for the delay or any message over the loudspeaker of how long it will be stopped. I have sat, just sat, for as long as an hour and a half. No reason to like any of this, except that the train, being transportation between Chilton and New York, is neither of these places, and, thus, comparatively better. I do a lot of thinking on the train.

I am thinking, today, about why I have always expected my parents to get divorced, and how odd it is that they haven't already, that it's taken them so long (and who knows if they'll even go through with it this time, though I think they will). I am also thinking, on the train, about Uncle Jay, and his funeral, and his eulogy, which was delivered by my father, and the gathering after his funeral, which was held in Chilton at our house.

"Is the wake going to be here?" I asked Katherine, when the arrangements were being discussed Friday.

"I don't think you could technically call it a wake, since Jay's body won't be here," Katherine said, with the appearance of giving the matter great thought. Yet I knew that the thoughtfulness was actually directed toward working out the arrangements, that her seeming concern for the correct word was just reflexive. "I guess it would be called a gathering, just a gathering, of his friends and Pat's, here after the funeral."

My mother is an editor, and precise about words always. I admire this. My father, a writer, admires it, too, except when she does it in the middle of an argument—which I doubt she can even help. But then it would infuriate him. Anything she did then would set him off. "Wake, gathering, for Christ's sweet sake what the hell does it matter, you know what I meant!" he might have screamed at her if she had given him the answer she gave me, if they were, just in that moment, in a bad time together. If they were in a good one, though, he might just as well have said, "I don't know what you'd call it, hmmm, let's see . . ." and either gone to look it up in the dictionary himself or asked me to check.

And I'm thinking about Katherine, too, my mother, the one everyone wants. Including me. Yes. True. But not the way everyone else does, or thinks they do. I'm thinking about her. I always think about her.

At the gathering after the funeral, to which everyone who had been at the funeral came (except Walter, despite his having delivered the eulogy), a whole feast was set out at the same long, dark-oak table from which Walter, one Sunday when I was a kid, swept off all the china and glass and silverware within his long arm's reach onto the floor, enraged beyond endurance by something I have either forgotten or never known. But now the table stood, not set for a family, but arrayed for a buffet. My mother had made some of the food, some had been delivered by a catering service, and some had been brought by my mother's best friend, Dorothy Fiori, who lives across the street. In the refrigerator, I knew, for later, was a small casserole of Dorothy Fiori's famous lasagna, made solely for me. I appreciated that. At the center of the table there was a giant pink ham, with yellow pineapple rings and bright, blood-red cherries stabbed onto toothpicks. I hate ham, dead pink pig meat. Too salty, too dead, too pink.

My mother said to me, "I'm trying to keep Aunt Pat drunk today, for medicinal purposes. If you see her glass is empty, would you refill it if I'm not around? I'll have a bottle of Scotch near her."

"Is keeping her drunk a good idea? How will she get over it if she doesn't get to feel sad?" I asked. I had read an Elisabeth Kübler-Ross book, *On Death and Dying*, about a month before, I don't know why. Kübler-Ross talks a lot about the importance of grieving.

Though I genuinely meant my question, it sounded artificial coming out of my mouth, even to me.

My mother sighed deeply as if with bottomless and inexpressible irritation, pulling her lips back. "For God's sake, Elizabeth, I have twenty-five or thirty people here. I don't have time to debate philosophy!"

And of course she had a point.

But so did I.

That's the problem—one of them.

To say my mother is under pressure now hardly begins to describe it. She looks as if she could pull apart in the middle, like dough rolled out and stretched so thin that it becomes transparent and breaks. The skin around her mouth is tight. She has been helping my aunt help my uncle die. She is probably about to get divorced. She is senior editor of the children's book department of Rahleigh and Byrd Publishers, a "distinguished New York house," as I have often seen it referred to in magazine articles about her.

She has me.

I shouldn't have said anything.

Both my father and I tend to say whatever is on our minds. We are honest and spontaneous, if you look at it one way; we are tactless and insensitive if you look at it in another. My mother holds things in; her instinct is that other people should do the same, like wanting to keep Aunt Pat drunk instead of letting her feel sad. My mother is tactful and aware of other people or she's dishonest and repressed; again, how do you look at it—how do *I* look at it, especially when I can see it either way and both angles of vision have their reasonable points?

Walter and I are both Sagittarians, busy shooting our arrows in the air—they fall to earth we know not where—occasionally stabbing someone, though usually unintentionally (well, some of Walter's stabs are certainly intentional). Katherine, a Cancer, holds on tight with her crab claws; she never lets go, and she always, always moves sideways. You can never be sure what she means from her words, for all her precision in picking just the right ones; you have to be on the lookout for other signals.

When my father swept the dishes from the table that time, we all sat there for what seemed to me like a long time, stock-still, frozen after that huge violence of sound. Like a snapshot, I see us shocked into silence: Walter, Katherine, me, my brother Steph (nine years older than me and now in the army). We could not have sat still for as long, as quietly, as I remember.

At last my mother stood up and, kneeling on the floor, began to pick up the shattered pieces of glass and china, the plates still coated with a sheen of gravy, the shards of glass still wet, the ice cubes unbroken but melting on the floor.

But, however big I am on honesty and free Sagittarian expression, I am not as big—in any sense—as Camille Blanche Peckinpaker, hereafter known as Cam, who writes her best-selling young-adult novels, edited by my mother, under the more sophisticated name of C. B. Peck. Cam was also at the gathering-not-a-wake, for God only knows what reason. Well, I know what reason. She wanted to "be supportive of your mother." What she really wanted was to be *adopted* by my mother. I know: She tells me so at every opportunity, snaking chummily up to me and saying with vitriolic sweetness, "You know, I'm just *so* jealous of you, Elizabeth. I want Katherine to be *my* mother."

"She likes you too, Cam, very much, and I know she loves working with you. She often mentions it."

Instead of: Go away, leave me alone, you big baby.

You don't have any *idea* what it's like to be Katherine's daughter. True, she mentions you a lot, but you would not enjoy knowing what those mentions are. Though she genuinely admires your writing, as I do. But you personally drive her bananas, as you do me.

Katherine is a very good and famous editor of children's books. She's edited many classic children's books, by many famous authors, and she has won a number of awards for "editorial excellence." There is a whole shelf of books by the fireplace in the living room that grateful authors have dedicated to her, their loving words printed in every copy of their books, valentines for the world to see. "To my darling Katherine." "For Katherine, without whom this book would not exist." "To Katherine, who showed me the way to the kingdom." There are also five shelves of autographed books, sometimes with little drawings or sketches if the author who signed the book was also an illustrator. For instance, there's Edmund Weller, the author-artist of the Jeremiah Bear books, whom my mother discovered when we were on vacation in Cape Cod. He was sketching children playing on the beach and she sneaked up and took one look at his pad.

"Oh, this was no *ordinary* beach scene; he had made all the children even smaller than they were, there were no adults around, and they were dwarfed rather comically by this very, very *large* beach ball they were all playing with—it was practically a picture book in itself, and very funny." Katherine gave him her business card, out of a cloisonné business-card holder that was given to her by another author—she was carrying her purse, we were just walking along the beach, not going for a swim, we had just arrived—and she told him to call her in New York, at Rahleigh and Byrd. He did, and she worked with him for about a year, and talked to him, and took him out to lunches at fancy places when he was dead broke—he always made a big deal about the lunches later, when he became famous—and looked at book after book of sketches and eventually he came up with Jeremiah Bear.

"And I took *one look,"* says Katherine, her voice still exultant after all these years, genuinely exultant, not phony, not put on for librarians or interviewers, "and I knew, I knew he'd found his voice and his eye, to say and to show the things that I always *felt*—felt, because one never *knows,* and that's why publishers have to be willing to take risks, to trust their intuition—that Edmund, and *only* Edmund, had to say, and to show, in a touching and beautiful and funny and unique way, a way that's of course his and his alone." And the happy ending is he's since done eleven books about Jeremiah Bear and they've been translated all over the world and won zillions of awards and made a mint for both Edmund Weller and Rahleigh and Byrd.

These are the kind of stories, and there are many more and they're all kind of wonderful, that they always tell about my mother, whom they call "apocalyptic" and "visionary" in the same breath that they call R&B "a distinguished New York house"; although, to me, R&B will always, always be rhythm and blues, not Rahleigh and Byrd, rhythm and blues and Murray the K and Tabby and me—but that's another story. Anyway, Edmund Weller's inscriptions always include little visual puns on the word "bear," like, "To Katherine, for (little sketch of Jeremiah) -ing with me again," or "For Katherine, to whom I (little sketch of Jeremiah) my soul."

Most of the inscriptions, though, are unillustrated. "Katherine, you gave me the key, Renaldo." "With thanks and love, Cy." And, from Camille Blanche

Peckinpaker, "Katherine, somebody lied: I'm sure you're *really* my mother. Love, your Cam."

"Oh, that Cam, that Cam, she is going to drive me ab-so-lute-ly craaaaaazy," I have heard my mother say many, many times. Often, when Cam calls at home—all Katherine's authors have her home phone number—I watch my mother wring her hands, grimace, and roll her eyes, her jaw tight with tension and exasperation, all the while saying, in those tones of reassurance and gentle encouragement for which she is well-known, "Umm-hmm . . . well, Cam dear, just go back to the typewriter and work at it, that's the only solution, it will come. Oh, I forgot, the typewriter's in the shop. . . ." She turns to me with an extra wring of the hands. "No, no, Cam, don't waste your time trying to borrow one now if it's going to be ready Monday; just work, just sit in that lovely apartment of yours with no one but Mehitabel and Sly for company" (Cam's cat and golden retriever), "take the phone off the hook, and go over the manuscript. Yes. That's right. Just think. Umm-hmm. Umm-hmm. It will come. It will. Now, Cam dear, you know you always feel this way at this point in a manuscript. Yes. Umm-hmm, you do. It will pass, Cam, it will, I promise! No, no, just in longhand, until the typewriter is ready Monday. It's the thinking part that's important now. Well, do you have a felt-tip marker, then, Cam?" and so on.

When she hangs up the phone after such a call it is with a violence that almost equals my father's. Katherine does not wish she were Cam's mother. "God knows, God *knows*," says Katherine, "I find it hard enough being her editor."

The thing is, though, Cam is a good writer; I like her books myself. "Poor Cam," says my mother. "She wouldn't be that way if she could help it, and she's in therapy.'' I know Cam's story from my mother; I feel sorry for her myself, much as I dislike her; she's had a terrible life. Her parents died in a car wreck when she was six; she was beaten by her foster mother and molested by her foster father when she reached puberty. When she was fifteen she made a suicide attempt; when she came to, her foster mother said to her, ''Camille, so help me God if you ever try that again I'll cut off both your arms and beat you with the bloody stumps.''

A marked contrast to what awaited me.

It's no wonder Cam is so overweight, I'd guess at least a hundred pounds overweight.

''She's quite open about admitting that she is building a wall of fat between herself and the world,'' my mother has said. ''Can you blame her, after all she's been through?'' No, not blame, but probably that's another reason she's jealous of me. I'm sure she thinks I'm thin. Not that I think so. I think I'd look a whole lot better if I lost ten or fifteen pounds; but compared to Cam, I guess I'm thin.

But still, what do you say when one of your mother's best-selling authors, who weighs, conservatively, two hundred and twenty pounds and is thirty-six years old, tells you she *wants* your mother? Compassion or no compassion, it's a difficult situation, especially right after your uncle's funeral, when your parents are on the verge of divorce and you yourself are only just back from a very, very strange place.

''I know she cares a lot about you too, Cam,'' I said. ''My mother always speaks highly of you.'' This was not what I felt like saying nor was it, exactly, the truth, but it was exactly what my mother would have wanted me to say. After that sigh when I suggested that keeping Aunt Pat drunk wasn't such a good idea, after that sigh and the look that accompanied it, a look of concentrated frustration and rage, not at me particularly but somehow crammed into a spot way too small for it, after that, I owed my mother something.

But at least I was able to add, honestly and of my own volition, "I really liked *Fortune Street,* by the way, Cam."

Fortune Street was Cam's last novel, and one thing I'll say for Cam is she can really write great depressing autobiographical novels. *Fortune Street* is about this kid whose parents are killed in a boating accident when he is five and he has to go live with his aunt and uncle, who have one other boy, and the aunt and uncle's whole focus is on their own little boy who as it turns out is a real rotten, bad-apple character—lying and manipulative and a thief and of course he eventually gets into dope and trouble. But the aunt and uncle pour out all this love and affection on him and shoot him all kinds of slack while they're hard disciplinarians and unaffectionate and unfair to the kid they've been forced to adopt and really just wanted for his money which it turns out there wasn't that much of but they were stuck with him anyway. Of course, the adopted kid turns out to be the good kid, kind and compassionate and bright. And he keeps trying to win their love, but no go. It sounds like melodrama, and it is, but it's *good* melodrama. I couldn't put it down. Every time I pick up one of Cam's books I always start out prejudiced against it because of her; but she's such a good writer you can't help but be sucked into it.

"Thanks," Cam said.

"What are you working on now?" I asked her. I have learned that this is the polite way to ask authors about their work, having seen my father once fly into a rage when asked, "Are you working on anything now?" by a perfectly innocent, nice lady who was waiting for the same commuter train that we were at the Chilton station, my father and I waiting for my mother, the lady for her husband.

"Madam," said my father, drawing himself to his full height (and he's six foot two anyway), "Madam . . ." and his icy rage got a few degrees chillier (already the lady was moving back a bit) " . . . to ask an author if he is 'working on anything' is roughly analogous to asking if he is still male, if he still has his penis. He is *always* working, always, whether the world realizes it or not, whether it approves or not, whether it sees or is blind, whether it praises or scorns. Do you understand?"

"Yes," she said, backing away farther, adding in a soothing tone, "Perfectly. Perfectly." She nodded politely and gave us a pleasant smile, then turned away and stared down the tracks in the direction the train would come.

Later, when I asked my mother about this, as she was tucking me into bed that night, after I'd described the whole episode, she said, "Oh, really, that is inexcusable, he has no right . . . though of course it's true, a writer *is* always at work. But to give that woman—oh, and I bet it was Mrs. Fancher, too, Al Fancher comes in on that same train as I do, oh dear—to give that poor woman a *lecture*, really, he has no right. I know he's had a bad day, but that was inexcusable."

It had been a bad day because Walter had had a rejection letter on an assignment he'd done, a profile of a woman named Dyl Featherstone, a Hollywood astrologer, "Star-reader to the Stars"; and, in addition, just as he was trying to recover from that by getting started on another piece of writing, an aluminum-siding salesman had telephoned, interrupting a train of thought and ruining his concentration for the afternoon, so he had given up writing for the day and gone down to the living room to lie on the couch, read magazines, listen to Thelonious Monk on the stereo headphones, smoke cigarette after cigarette and drink Johnny Walker Red until it was time to go pick up my mother at the train station. After Katherine tucked me in, I heard them fighting about it, the murmur of angry voices with the sudden loud explosions of "GODDAMNIT!" and "FOR CHRIST'S SWEET SAKE!" from my father reaching me as I lay in bed.

"What am I working on?" repeated Cam to me at the gathering after the funeral. "Oh, something about child sexual abuse, a girl who's just hit puberty is molested by an older male relative—I'm not ready to talk about it too much."

If a writer is always working—and I'm still not sure of that—then I am working right now, sitting on the train, remembering Sunday and who said what and how I felt. But how can it be "working" if I'm not actually writing anything? Is it enough to be remembering and *want* to write? Because that I do, I definitely do. But I can't imagine ever being able to turn depressing things in my real life into writing half as well as Cam. Lately, I can't seem to write anything at all. For a while I was working on this poem. "In Transit" it was supposed to be called, about the train and not being part of, or at least not feeling part of, anything on either end, so that only the traveling was real. But I just couldn't get it and I put it aside. But every time I'm on the train, like now, no matter how many other things I might be thinking about, I always think of "In Transit" and I wonder if I'll ever get back to that poem and make it something good or if it's just a stupid idea in the first place and I should forget about it. If I got mugged in New York and the mugger pushed me onto the subway tracks, enraged that I had so little cash on me or maybe just for the hell of it, I bet the last thought I would have, in the split second before I hit the hot rail and got electrocuted, would be about "In Transit," and I would regret that I had left it unfinished. But even knowing that is not enough to get me working on it again. How is it that I can want to do something as badly as I want to write, and not do it?

As I gaze out the dirty, breathed-on-by-too-many-people window of the train, only half-seeing the view I have seen hundreds of times before, I find myself wishing I had known Uncle Jay better. A gruff man with a cigar almost continually in his mouth, he ran an import business. When I was very young, his manner terrified me; stroking my hair, for instance, on several occasions he grabbed a handful of it—though always gently—and, brandishing the long-bladed scissors he kept on his desk, said, "How 'bout a haircut, Lizzie?" Eventually, of course, I came to realize he was kidding, and came to understand his underlying kindness, even indulgence, toward Pat, my mother, and me, his "zussies," or sweets, as he called us. Once, when I was very little, maybe seven, I was visiting him and Pat at the import showroom, one floor of a building, a large, dusty space with glass cases and piles of cardboard boxes and desks heaped high with sheafs of papers. I came upon some small brass boxes in one of the cases, pillboxes actually. Several had tiny, perfect enameled pictures on their hinged tops: a gondola, with the gondolier in the striped shirt pushing it along a canal; a stylized rose, complete with tiny thorns. One had a mother-of-pearl top, another a top of cut, faceted blue glass, like a giant sapphire—eight different designs altogether. The minute I saw them I knew they'd be perfect for my dolls, for jewelry boxes. The dolls were orphans who lived an adventurous and happy life in an institution which was half orphanage, half boarding school, run by a kind and compassionate older doll named Miss Flora in an open bookshelf along one side of my bedroom. I played with these dolls in their elaborate, novelistic kingdom, until I was almost thirteen, when I went away to Lakeland, a private school in Massachusetts which I was later thrown out of, as was my best friend there, Tabitha Whittaker, also known as Tabby, Tab, and occasionally Tabbins.

Jay gave me one each of the eight pillboxes, and I set one on each of the bedside tables I had made of cardboard beside eight dolls' beds (three dolls didn't get jewelry boxes; they each shared with one of the ones that did). Each doll had particular tiny treasures: Several had twigs of shiny coral, given to me by Katherine before she had her broken coral necklace restrung; most had a seashell or two or a bit of smooth, polished beach glass, or a tiny necklace I'd made of Indian beads. I imagined Sandy, the doll who was a tomboy, and to whom the box with gondola had gone (an anonymous donor, a philanthropist, had sent the boxes to the orphanage; everything that happened to the dolls had to have a motive. Does this mean I will be a novelist?)—anyway, I could picture Sandy running her hands over the gondola jewelry box each night before she went to sleep: and then, when she slept, stiff eyelids with their stiff, long black lashes closed over glass eyes, she dreamed of Venice, which Miss Flora had told all the dolls about. Uncle Jay had made it possible for Sandy to dream about Venice, though of course he hadn't the faintest idea of having done this.

Now I use two of the pillboxes for vitamins, which I keep in my purse, along with contact-lens stuff and clean underpants, in case I don't spend the night at home. I take seventeen vitamins, twice a day, because I'm on vitamin therapy. One round of vitamins fills up two pillboxes. I was playing with those dolls only four years ago. I told Tabby once, in jest—because it wasn't even true at the time I said it, which she knew—"I played with dolls until I started giving head." A practice we both agreed, then, sounded disgusting, but she said, "Save that line, Liz, save it till you're thirty and jaded; think how handy it'll be and how clever your lovers will think you are." I'm seventeen now. Tabby and I were both barely fifteen when we had this conversation, and eager, we said, to be jaded. Seventeen now—a pill for each year, though I doubt that's how Dr. Prewitt figured it out. Why does it seem so long ago?

And now my Uncle Jay is dead.

I don't have much to remember him by. Those boxes. The extremely foul cigars he smoked, his cigar-smelling kisses, his ashtray with a hinged brass lid on it. When I'd just learned to read Jay asked me one day to read him the book I had under my arm, a Dr. Seuss book called *A Fly Went By.* I did it happily, delightedly, as I remember—I must've been seven, eight at the most. But then, when I was nine, ten, eleven, twelve, he'd always ask me to read *A Fly Went By* or ask me if I remembered that time I read it to him; and soon I got embarrassed and made excuses not to visit him, which would have happened anyway because he was aging and getting sicker and sicker and they didn't let kids my age into the hospital. He had cancer, and his left leg, which had gotten slammed accidentally in a taxi door, ulcerated and never healed. Then, when he was getting close to death, he began to ask repeatedly for apples, Arkansas Black Twig apples, a variety he remembered from his boyhood on a rice farm in Arkansas. I never heard him do this, but Katherine told me, and for some reason it tore me up. I somehow could *feel* that more than I could his cancer and his dying and his pain. My aunt, emptying that reeking lidded ashtray, stood by him and put up with him as he ran off five different nurses (according to Katherine) by insulting them (two of them, again according to Katherine, with racial epithets). But my aunt couldn't lessen his pain, and she couldn't procure for him the variety of apple that, by the end, he wept for.

My mother says that Jay was very dashing when he used to call for Pat when they were courting. She says he always wore a white carnation in his lapel, and that Pat told her he was a marvelous dancer.

Later on in the afternoon of the funeral, Camille Blanche Peckinpaker began scarfing down these meringue cookies that Dorothy Fiori from across the street had made. On three separate occasions that day, I heard her saying, in the swooningly dramatic way she has, "Oh! I think these cookies are the best thing I *ever* ate in my *entire mouth!*"

That was Cam's attempt at wit. Entire *life* is what you'd expect her to say and she says entire *mouth.*

On the other hand, she's a very, very good writer. And, as I kept reminding myself after the funeral, and, as I remind myself now, thinking as I commute into school, as the train passes a factory where huge wooden spools are stacked outdoors, she did have a difficult childhood.

On the other hand, who *didn't* have a difficult childhood?

I don't know where to draw the line, which side to look at things from, how to measure, how to decide. About Cam, about my parents, about anything. I don't know anything—and yet at this very moment I am clackety-clacking my way into New York to attend this dumb progressive school, MABEE, where I think they know even less than I do, indicated by the fact that both MA-

BEE's staff and principal (though calling Sid Meyerhoff a principal hardly seems accurate) say, "Thank you for sharing that," about twenty times a day.

The train has just pulled into the tunnel; ten minutes of complete dark outside the windows until (I assume, like everyone else) we'll arrive at Grand Central. But I can't stop thinking about yesterday: my Aunt Pat laughing, dazed, glass full, eyes full, everyone trying so hard to cheer her up; these huge blue eyes of hers filled with uncried tears, which made her eyes sing blueness. She's a very pretty woman, sixty-one, eight years older than my mother. My mother has always been jealous of Aunt Pat's looks. My mother doesn't see, refuses to see, how pretty she herself is, with green eyes the color of green sea glass, perfect skin, a soft, yielding quality. They're both lovely, I think, though my aunt has this tilt to her jaw sometimes, stubborn, hard, unyielding. She has no children. Still, my aunt says, "Thank you," if you compliment her on her eyes or her skin or the way she looks in a particular shade. My mother just goes "Tchh," grimaces, and makes a self-deprecating gesture with her hands raised to her face, as if warding off any praise that should mistakenly come to it.

Everyone's always jealous of someone. Cam, of me. My mother, of Aunt Pat or at least of her looks. But I think Aunt Pat is also jealous of my mother, of her being an award-winning editor and having articles written about her and all that.

Which I know Katherine doesn't even want. How could she? Whenever she has to give a speech she has insomnia for about a week before. She practices and practices and practices the speech, saying it into a tape recorder, but each time her voice gets softer and sort of more locked in her throat (and the more she goes crazy over it, the more irritated my father gets. "GODDAMN-

IT, Katherine, just do it! Just DO it, for Christ's sweet sake! If you didn't obsess over it all the goddamn time you wouldn't have this problem! If I have to listen to that goddamn speech one more time . . ." and so on).

What my mother *says* is that she wants to write novels. She wants to write novels, but she doesn't have the time. "I have this box of things I've been saving, to go through, and I think if I can find time to string them together, and then, from there . . . No, but why even think about it; I won't have time, not till September—and in September Dorothy Fiori is having that foot surgery, and she's going to need help for at least a month and a half. Then there's Thanksgiving, and then Christmas, and if I'm *possibly* going to have anything done for the fall list—I have a Weller on that one, and one of Cam's, and a novel by W. W. Spelling, and Renaldo Sant'Angelo . . . oh, the color plates from that are being shipped air freight from Rome and everything *has* to go like clockwork. And then there's, oh God, there's sales conference."

She says she'd write novels if she had the time, novels and poetry for adults. "So, goddamnit, Katherine, take the time!" thunders my father. "But Walter," says Katherine, "my authors. How would you feel if Michael left Simon & Schuster to go off and write a novel?" But to me she says she had no choice, she had to go to work because Walter was "financially unstable" and "I had two small children and I couldn't live with the financial insecurity" and "I chose editing because it was the closest thing to writing, and of course there are *some* things I like about it." But she never elaborates on the things she likes. And she doesn't have two small children now; Steph's gone and I'm seventeen. If she wanted to quit I would work in a bookstore or something—she doesn't have to stay there for me. So why doesn't she leave?

"No, no," Katherine says, "Elizabeth, I'm very touched that you would offer, but—well, there are reasons that I can't go into with you, but it just wouldn't work for, oh, for many reasons. I *do* need to continue working there."

But what about the year my father had a best seller, why did she edit then? My father, who lives in New York now, is also a writer. Walter writes Hollywood biographies and profiles of comedians and show-business personalities and musicians and actors, and the people who look after them, like their managers, astrologers, shrinks, bartenders, rabbis, masseurs, and acupuncturists. And he had, one year, the year I was eight, I think, that one best seller, about a famous actor and actress, a married couple. One review that year called him "The Boswell of Broadway," and he started referring to himself as Boz for a while at parties. (I could hear him; many of the parties that year were at our house.) I didn't know who Boswell was. Walter wouldn't tell me; he wanted me to look it up. Boswell, James, 1740–1795, Scottish lawyer and writer; biographer of Samuel Johnson. I didn't know who Samuel Johnson was, either. ("You don't know who *Samuel Johnson* is? What do they teach you in school, anyway? Jesus Christ, look Samuel Johnson up too.")

That was the year that, besides his telling jokes in a Scottish accent at parties, we had a whole lot of money, or so I was told. "I'm very, very proud of your father," said Katherine—but she didn't quit Rahleigh and Byrd to write her own novel. He wrote; she edited and supported. Supported him, supported us; in a different way, supported her authors. Kneeled in the glass, picked up the shards.

* * *

After the funeral, when my aunt's glass and her blue eyes were never empty, and the skin around my mother's mouth was stretched so tightly I could almost see the blue veins under it, and Camille Blanche Peckinpaker was pigging out on cookies, there was a point, after I had heard Cam say her cookie line twice, when I thought I was going to throw up. I went to the upstairs bathroom. Dorothy Fiori, my mother's best friend, was just coming out. She said, "How are you holding up, Elizabeth?"

I said, "Okay, I guess." Then I said, "Cam Peckinpaker just told me again how much she wishes Katherine were her mother."

"Oh, that," Dorothy Fiori laughed. "Listen, doll, you have the mother everyone wants. You know that."

I went into the bathroom, but I couldn't throw up; so I went to my bedroom and lay down for a few minutes. The liquor cabinet is in the pantry directly underneath my bedroom, and I could hear the bottles being slid in and out. I thought about calling Jonathan, my sort-of boyfriend from school, who lives in Riverdale, but I decided against it. I also thought of calling my father.

During the time at the funeral home yesterday when everybody was milling around before the memorial service for Jay, my father asked me if I wanted to come with him while he got a drink. I said sure, and Walter and I left the funeral home and went down the street, to a bar around the corner, one of those with a lot of dark oak panels and mirrors behind the bar. It was the kind of room you associate with night; it looked odd with all the bright, eleven-o'clock-in-the-morning sunlight streaming in above the café curtains.

My father said to the bartender, "Thank God you're open. Extra-dry martini with a twist of lemon peel."

The bartender, a middle-aged, slightly plump man, gave it to him, then said, "Haven't I seen you here before? Wait, don't tell me." He closed his eyes for a second and put one finger to his forehead. He had a pleasant voice, with just the faintest trace of an Irish accent to it. "Yes!" he said. "Three, four years ago, about this time of day . . . I b'lieve it was, let's see, your mother-in-law's funeral, am I right?"

"Yes, yes!" said my father excitedly. "My God, Liz, did you hear that? What a memory!"

"I never forget a face," said the bartender. "Never."

"Were you there, at Grandma Eleanor's funeral?" Walter asked me. "I can't remember."

"No, I was at Lakeland then, remember? You guys wrote me about it after it had already happened."

"Oh, right, right," said Walter, then added to the bartender, "This is my daughter, Elizabeth."

"Sure, and she's a beautiful girl," said the bartender, drawing "girl" into two syllables, "gurr—rrul." "You must be very proud of her."

When we went back up to the funeral home, they were almost ready for the service. I sat with my mother and Aunt Pat. My father sat in the front so he could get up to deliver the eulogy after the rabbi spoke. It was odd, in a way, that they (I guess it was Katherine and Pat) should have asked him to do the eulogy, for to my knowledge he and Jay were at best mistrustful. Yet, in the middle of his talk—"for Jay and I shared the closest bond that two men can share, and that is we were married to two sisters"—he had to turn away from the microphone, shaken with sobs. Then he composed himself, and continued. I was afraid; I knew he wasn't crying for Jay, but for another death. I couldn't then, and I can't now, think about that too much.

Outside the dirty window of the train it is still dark. That's another thing I can't think about too much: being so far under the earth, in the dark, in a hole with countless tons of concrete and buildings and streets and cars and people above. But that, at least, I know how to not think about.

When I was lying on the bed on Sunday at the gathering after the funeral, people milling around downstairs, I thought about calling my father, but I vetoed that too.

From my bedroom that day (only yesterday, but it already seems long ago) I listened to the noise of the people below, the talking and laughter and voices, the clinking of ice in glasses. From up above, it sounded like any old party, like the parties that year my father had his one best seller. No one would have known that this one was caused by the death of an old man who had cried for apples as he lay dying, who had once worn carnations and given his niece eight pillboxes for her dolls, who had been an excellent dancer.

After a while I got up and went back downstairs, just in time to hear Cam Peckinpaker announce for the third time, to yet another group of people, "These cookies are the most delicious thing I ever ate in my *entire* mouth!" Everyone around her laughed appreciatively.

But now it's time for me to stop thinking about all this. Lights have come on outside the filthy window. The train has made it through the tunnel, all the trusting souls on it jerked safely into Grand Central Station. I'm in New York now.

I have the mother everyone wants.

I have been lonely all my life.

Two

Frozen Yogurt and a Kiwi Fruit

JONATHAN, my sort-of boyfriend, and I went to see an experimental Italian movie after school today. It's Monday, a week and a day after Jay's funeral, another gray, cold, rainy November day.

I didn't like the movie; even before we went I knew I wouldn't. I like movies with definite plots, good guys and bad guys, witty dialogue. I like the old thirties screwball romantic comedies with a lot of good old-fashioned sexist flirtation and banter, where love manages to conquer all, though only just barely and not till the end of the film. But I'm ashamed to admit this to anyone, let alone Jonathan, because I know very well how naïve those values are, expecting love to save you and so on; so I went with him to the stupid experimental Italian movie.

Afterward we walk around, and Jonathan critiques the movie. "In—*cred*—ible photography, don't you think? *Rilly* precise images, you know, but with that subtle, dreamlike quality of nuance. *Rilly* excellent." He always talks like this, which is why he is only my semi-semi-semi-boyfriend. On top of this, he is a vegetarian health-food person, and he pushes it all the time. Meat is pretty disgusting to me, and I would probably be a vegetarian myself right now if it weren't for him. But an afternoon with Jonathan fills me with an urgent need for salami, Italian sausage, hamburgers, chops, steaks, cutlets. Still, "Yes, Jonathan," "No, Jonathan," I say most of the time, keeping it simple or trying to.

Jonathan has this little gap between his two front teeth. He's not handsome, though he has a very nice body and a smile that would be winning if it weren't for that little gap. His hair, which is thick and brown and wavy, is a little long, but more as if he spaced out getting it cut than as if he is trying to be a latter-day hippie. Jonathan wants to go to bed with me. I keep saying no. I don't know why, since I probably will say yes eventually. I'm not playing hard to get; I'm not playing anything, but Jonathan doesn't inspire me.

So why do I hang around with him or let him hang around with me? It's just too much effort, at this point, to say buzz off, Jon, just like eventually it will be too much effort to keep saying, no, Jonathan, I don't want to sleep with you, no no no. One day I'll just give up and say oh, all right.

That's not the way they did it in the thirties movies, believe me.

Earlier in the school year, Adele, this girl who dyed her hair various colors, every week or so a different color and of course that included the turquoises and magentas (she's no longer here; she got caught sniffing coke in the bathroom and got thrown out), anyway, she and I used to jive about a school yearbook of our invention, to be called, tentatively, "MABEE Not." Mabee is our school, acronymically named for Meyerhoff Association for Behavioral and Emotional Education. You would think that somebody would have had the basic brains to see that such an acronym doesn't cut it, especially for an institution that is supposed to inspire confidence; but they take themselves very seriously around here, and nobody did. Actually, it is a pretty accurate description: Everything about MABEE is very vague. But just as Sidney Meyerhoff, whose brainchild MABEE is, can't see the inappropriateness of the name, he is equally blind to just how perversely appropriate it really is. He doesn't have much of a sense of humor. He doesn't have much sense period.

There're only about twelve kids here (give or take a few; turnover is rapid). Each of us is here because no place else would take us. Each and every MABEE student has been thrown out of somewhere or been in mental hospitals or gotten in trouble with the police or been on dope; we are all "problem adolescents." I'm not sure what Jonathan's problem is; he and I never talk about anything important; but I know he lived in California for a while. He's always saying things like, "I remember one day when I was at this head shop in Carmel," waiting for me to pick up on it and ask him when and why he was in California; but I never do. He might have run away from home when he was younger and gotten into some kind of trouble, or perhaps there was some big custody fight over him; I know his parents are divorced and he now lives with his mother and stepfather in Riverdale, New York. Anyway, you might think that with all the MABEEites being "troubled" (I mean, "troubled," who isn't? As Mose Allison, this great blues singer and piano player my father listens to all the time, or did when he lived with us, sings in one of his songs, "This world is just one big trouble spot. . . ."), anyway, you'd think, wouldn't you, that there'd be some kind of an automatic bond between us, if only in reaction to being continually urged to *own* our experiences, or share them. But there isn't. We're all basically in our own private galaxies here. I got along okay with Adele, for instance, but I haven't kept track of her since she left MABEE; I've hardly even thought of her. She and I did have fun, though, with "MABEE Not," the yearbook. It was going to be kind of a *National Lampoon* parody of yearbooks, peppered with a lot of jargon Sidney Meyerhoff and Co. are fond of using all the time, such as "How 'bout a warm fuzzie?" or "How does that make you *feel?"* or designating every "behavior" as "appropriate" or "inappropriate." Adele and I figured out great catty poses for all the MABEE students and faculty: Sidney Meyerhoff in a straitjacket lying on a psychiatrist's couch, a stuffed animal beside him, the psychiatrist a very bosomy *Cosmopolitan*-cover type with her legs crossed provocatively and showing lots of cleavage, and somehow, we hadn't figured out how yet, diet food worked in. Jonathan we planned to picture meditating in a lotus position while seated on the toilet. The toilet seat was Adele's idea: perfect. Wherever she is, and whatever color her hair is now, for sure Adele would be ashamed of my taking up with Jonathan.

"Is that fruit prepared with sugar?" asks Jonathan sternly. We're in a frozen-yogurt place on Third Avenue and Jonathan is surveying the choice of toppings behind the glass on the counter.

"Strawberries yes, pineapple no," says the kid behind the counter, who looks as weary as Jonathan looks disapproving. He's not unattractive, and not much older than Jon and me.

"But the pineapple is sugarless?"

"Yes."

"Is it fresh?"

"No, it's out of a can. The only thing fresh is the bananas for the banana splits."

"I'll take a banana, then."

"We don't *sell* just bananas, you got to take a split."

Jonathan sighs exaggeratedly, a reasonable man pushed beyond endurance, talking to an idiot, martyred by the absence of salable bananas. "Look," he says, very slowly, as if talking patiently to a dimwit, "just . . . sell . . . me . . . a . . . banana, okay?"

"Can't do it, man, don't you understand?" The counter guy is still cheerful, polite, but there's a definite edge. I'm on his side. "It's all counted out for the splits. There are rules here. You want a banana, buddy, buy a banana split or go to a market, you got it?"

Puffed with indignation, Jonathan opens his mouth to speak, but I touch his arm.

"Look, Jon, just keep me company while I have something, okay? Then we'll go buy you a banana somewhere. There're about a zillion fruit markets along Third."

"Oh, all right," says Jonathan, pouting. The kid behind the counter winks at me, and I smile back, which Jonathan completely misses because he's stalked away to go pout at a table. As I order a strawberry sundae I have a brief fantasy about the guy behind the counter, who looks maybe nineteen; brown hair, brown eyes, acne scars on his cheeks, tan corduroy pants under his white apron. He seems so normal, and I can't help wondering what it would be like to go out with some nice, normal guy. Go on dates. See recent-release American films on weekends instead of experimental Italian films on weekday afternoons. But then I chide myself: don't I, of all people, know that nobody is normal, no matter how they look? And what a generalization anyway, just because he works in a yogurt shop and wears cords. For all I know he could be translating Russian poetry at night. Besides, isn't it just as much a generalization to think that "normal," whatever that is, is good or desirable as it is to think that it's bad? With this thought, I suddenly realize how totally I have loused up a nice, simple little thirty-second fantasy by thinking too much. I get so sick of myself sometimes, it's just think, think, think all the time.

"Here's your sundae, miss." Mr. Maybe-Normal sets it down on the counter with the change. No chance for our hands to brush, our eyes to meet—that little wink and smile we shared while Jon was carrying on was it. No more interaction; this will not be a "meet-cute," as my father describes it, from a Hollywood movie. Now why am I even doing this? Do I really, with any little crumb of my mind, expect to find a savior or a romance, or, to put it in MABEE terms, a meaningful relationship in a Third Avenue yogurt shop?

I need to have a meaningful relationship with myself, that's who I need to have a meaningful relationship with. Very good, Elizabeth; you'll pull an *A* in Self-Understanding 101 for sure with insights like that.

I sit down at the table with Jonathan and begin spooning up the sundae. Vanilla frozen yogurt, reddish-brown mushy strawberries in syrup, white plastic spoon. I wonder why I ordered it. I eat it as Jonathan sulks.

"Want a bite?"

"Of that? No way," he says scornfully. I shrug and keep eating. "Well, maybe I'll have a taste."

I give him a spoonful.

"Not bad for a super-white-sugar-yin-freak-out-delight," he says.

We go outside and start walking down Third toward Forty-second Street, where Grand Central Station is. It's bitterly cold. I'm sorry I ate that stupid frozen yogurt. I'm cold right to my bones, right through my pea jacket. It is a gray slushy day, late on a gray afternoon, fourthirtyish, depressing. Jonathan takes my arm. I'm too cold to complain. We find a fruit market. Instead of buying a banana, Jonathan buys a kiwi fruit. We stand in the back of the fruit market near a heater and Jonathan methodically peels the brown hairy skin from his kiwi fruit with the red Swiss Army knife he always carries. Then he slices it, eating it slice by slice. He doesn't offer me any, but I wouldn't want it anyway.

Suddenly I feel combative. "How did you get to be such an authority on nutrition anyway, Jonathan?"

"I read. I pick up things."

"You mean you pick up books and read them? Are books the things that you pick up when you read? You know, that happens to me sometimes, too." Why am I doing this, why am I *bothering?* I never bug Jonathan, it isn't worth the trouble.

He ignores my behavior, though, or maybe he just doesn't notice it. "Yeah, Elizabeth, like that vitamin stuff you're on, that worries me. I just don't think you know what you're doing with that."

"Oh, yeah?" I was hearing voices till I started vitamin therapy, and food tasted funny, metallic. I have only to think of the symptoms list, in fact, to realize again just how far I have come with the vitamins. Dr. Prewitt gave me the list before she started me on the pills. *I often suffer from:* and then maybe fifty possibilities, each preceded by a little box. I went down the list, check, check, check. My hands were shaking really badly then; I had to use a large magic marker, I couldn't grip a regular-sized pen. Check, check, check. "Uncontrollable depression"; that was one that hit the nail on the head. I can't explain in words how that was different from what I feel now most of the time; but I know from the inside that it is different, right down to the marrow of my bones I know it.

But a writer has to try to explain in words.
But maybe I'm not a writer.

Of course, there were some symptoms I did not check off, boxes I could honestly leave blank. For instance, I remember one I wrote Tabby about: "I often feel animals are laughing at me." Tab and I had frequently discussed whether or not Hansel, the incredibly stupid golden retriever belonging to Lakeland's headmaster, Werner, was actually just pretending to be stupid and was in fact a highly trained intelligence dog, reporting on all illicit Lakeland activities to Werner. Tabby wrote me back a whole alternative symptom list: "I often suffer from the conviction that all golden retrievers are members of a conspiracy against me," and so on.

None of this, of course, is the kind of thing I generally tell people, any more than I do about cutting myself up back in Massachusetts, last year at Lakeland, where, as I may have mentioned, I first met Tabitha, who is now in a mental hospital herself.

All of this has run through my mind in the time it's taken for Jonathan to pop a few more slices of kiwi fruit into his mouth. He chews and swallows, licks his lips and continues, holding what's left of the slippery, wet, green, uneaten kiwi in his left hand, the Swiss Army knife in his right. "See, Elizabeth," he says earnestly, "those vitamins, if they're synthetic, they give your body a quick fix, like a drug, because they're not natural. And if you isolate just one or two nutrients and take a lot of them, without balancing them with all the others you need, *especially* if they're synthetic, you can wind up with an imbalance. Do you know if you take a whole complex, every single nutrient?"

I shrug, as if I neither know nor care. In fact, I know exactly what I take: how many milligrams of which vitamins, how often, what makes them go down easy, what makes them lump in my throat. And yes, Jonathan is right (he's smart, in his way, I'll give him that), it's not a complete complex, the vitamins are synthetic—but I've been over all that with Dr. Prewitt and I have no intention of discussing it with Jonathan anyway. Jonathan is the type of person who would use any information you gave him against you. Somehow, some way, he would, eventually.

"Besides, if you gave up meat and sugar, and ate more whole grains, fruits, and vegetables, and natural proteins like beans and nuts, you could get what you need just from your diet—you wouldn't need all those synthetic, plastic vitamin pills." Jonathan finishes his kiwi fruit. He licks his fingers and down his arm a bit where the juice dripped. Then he pulls on his gloves—leather, fur lined: Jonathan's vegetarianism does not extend to the outside of his body. All I can think of is how grotesque it is, damp, sticky fingers in fur-lined gloves.

Still, he's probably right about my diet. I can honestly feel meat isn't good for me. But sugar . . . I know sweets aren't good for me, but I enjoy them so much. And how much is there that I enjoy?

I don't enjoy experimental Italian movies.

I don't enjoy Jonathan.

"Come on, I have to catch the train," I say.

"Okay." Back out into the cold, arm in arm, Jon and I march down Third toward Grand Central.

I wonder what happened to Adele from MABEE. I didn't like her in the deep way I do Tabby; but still I felt we were allies at crazy MABEE. We had certain things in common, Adele and I. We used to talk about the mental hospitals we had been in—there was one we'd both been in, Grace Memorial, here in the city. I was first in one called Hurstview, in upstate New York, for about six weeks, then I got moved to Grace for about a month. Grace was where I got on the vitamins, under the care of Dr. Prewitt, whom I like pretty much. Adele had been in Payne-Whitney twice, then in Grace Memorial. Not at the same time I was there, but we both remembered the same overweight, kind but not-too-bright black night nurse. Also Adele was in some place on the West Coast for a while, and some place in New England—not Hurstview, but a name like Hurstview: Woodsmere, Greenfield, Knightsbridge—something like that, one of those pseudo-English-manor names. The place my friend and former Lakeland roommate Tabitha is now in is called Twelvetrees, one word. It's up somewhere near Boston, so I can't visit her, just write; and even that, lately, is getting to be nothing much.

It is cold and gray today. I cling to Jonathan, whom I don't even like.

At the station Jonathan walks me to my train, the same train he'd be taking to Riverdale if he were going home. But he isn't yet; he's going to some metaphysics lecture in the Village. He wanted me to come with him, but I couldn't bear it, the experimental Italian movie was more than enough. On the gray, dirty platform outside the train, he kisses me hard, squiggling his tongue all around my mouth.

He's a good kisser, I'll give him that. He's good at kissing.

"Why won't you let me make love to you?" he asks softly.

I shrug. The black guy is wheeling down the setup for the bar car. On every train between five and seven-thirty P.M. from New York out to Riverdale, Chilton, and beyond, there is a bar car. All the bartenders are black. All the conductors are white. It's not hard to guess the conductors get paid more.

Sometimes I think about problems, and it's as if all my problems, which appear so insoluble to me, are still just in a little tiny ring or circle that is me and my life; and then that circle is in another circle that's my family; and then there are more and more and more circles around me, around each person, circles that make one a particular race or religion, and then a member of a particular country, and a member of the world as a whole—circle after circle after circle, each person just encased in all his circles. Rings inside rings.

And it *all* just seems insoluble. And not just insoluble but also incomprehensible. For instance, I still don't understand about slavery, not really *understand* how people could take other people captive and take them away to another country and actually imagine that they could *buy* and *sell* them; human beings, little children, sometimes even (because from what I've read the white male owners often used to sleep with their black slave women and of course the women couldn't do anything about it)—sometimes their *own children* they'd buy and sell and beat! How can anyone understand such a thing? How can it have existed? It's one of those things—the Holocaust is another one—that I *know* happened and I think about a lot and yet I just can't believe it, can't believe people would do that to other people, *could* do that, and that it really happened.

Whenever I think about things like this, about slavery, about the Holocaust, about the circles, I start feeling guilty, because, really, I have so much. I'm a very advantaged person, and though none of it has made me happy I feel that it certainly *ought* to, in comparison to others who have so little. A few weeks ago, for instance, I saw this Puerto Rican girl on the IRT one morning as I rode down to MABEE. She couldn't have been more than fourteen, although she looked about twelve, and she was wearing this red, very old, plush coat with a fake-fur collar that was open because she couldn't get it around her big pregnant belly which was pressed against some kind of cotton print smock—no sweater, nothing warm, even though it was one of these cold, gray, wet days New York has been having this year seemingly without end. She had her arms crossed about her belly and this sad, vacant look on her face, and bad skin. I got off before she did. I can still see her face. And what if I were her? (I could have been, in some ways; I didn't use any kind of contraceptive a couple of times when I had sex.) But what if I had not only gotten pregnant, by, let's say, Gary, my Lakeland boyfriend, but had also not had my life of basically middle-class privilege? What if I had the same biochemically based schizophrenia that I do now but was pregnant with no money and no education, no two parents who, crazy as they are and on the brink as they are, still love me deeply? What would have happened to me? Who in the world would have found and gotten me onto vitamin therapy?

As it was, with all I have going for me, it was a close call.

But then again I am guessing about that girl's life, and maybe I'm completely wrong. Maybe what I thought was sadness was just quiet contemplation. Maybe she is a lot older than she looks. Maybe she is really twenty-six and married to a nice guy, maybe—whether she's married or not—she wanted the baby very much. There is no denying that she was poor, from the way she dressed; but maybe, because she's lived with it all her life, being poor doesn't bother her as much as it would me (but that's a thought I'm uncomfortable with, it's too self-serving). Maybe she thought the coat was a beautiful shade of red; maybe her mother—who will help her take care of the baby while she goes to work and to night school—gave it to her and so it has sentimental value to her.

Maybe she has hope.

When I ride with my mother home from New York on the train, she always has a bourbon from the bar car. A Wild Turkey. (Dorothy Fiori gave her some Wild Turkey last Christmas and the gift tag said, "A bird that does not fly.") She sinks into her seat with that bourbon, looking so tired, and she sighs a long sigh, which I guess to be part relief at not being at work anymore but also part weighted-down-ness at having so much work to think about still; more thoughts "swirling and swirling in my head," as she sometimes says, than there are papers and books in her attaché case, which is always loaded so full the zipper is never zipperable.

My mother has a whole vocabulary of sighs.

I feel more than sorry for her, I feel . . . devastated by her. *For* her. She is so sad. She works so hard. There is nothing I can do to make her happy. She loves me. Too much. Much more, but with so many more difficulties, than she does her authors. It's complicated. Whenever I meet her authors, even the ones that are much saner and more fun to be around than Cam Peckinpaker, they always say things like, "You're so *lucky* to have Katherine for a mother!"

And I am, but not in the way they think, or the way I imagine they think. I suspect I would *enjoy* my mother more, not love more but *enjoy* more, if she were just my editor or friend. Maybe it's as hard to be loved too much as too little.

I basically feel communication is impossible between two people anyway. There are all those rings; everything is so complicated. And how much you *want* to communicate seems to have nothing to do with it. Walter and Katherine truly wanted to work it out, both of them, but it was just impossible for them.

If my father is with her on the train, my mother will order a scotch and soda instead of bourbon. My father thinks bourbon is déclassé; they had a fight about it after Dorothy Fiori gave Katherine that Wild Turkey last Christmas. My father will knock back three or four extra-dry martinis with a twist of lemon (as I have heard him order in innumerable restaurants over the years, as I heard him order from the Irish bartender Sunday before last, at Jay's funeral, although his preferred at-home beverage is straight-up Johnny Walker Red). Three or four martinis between New York and Chilton, a trip of forty-five minutes.

My father is not in such hot shape.

Neither is Tabby, my old friend from Lakeland, which sounds like another mental hospital but is the boarding school she and I attended, the school where we were roommates, when we jived about Hansel, the golden retriever, where we hitchhiked into Lenox or Stockbridge together a couple of times a week for fresh apple cider and doughnuts in the fall, and for red licorice whips in the winter; no sooner would we step back outside from the warmth of the penny-candy store into winter New England than the soft sweet strands would turn crisp and brittle, as we walked down the snowy main street back toward the highway to school under the gray sky. And hot-fudge sundaes we would go for any time of the year that the urge struck us. Tabitha always ordered her sundaes with coffee ice cream instead of vanilla, because she had read somewhere that coffee ice cream had fewer calories than any other kind of ice cream. No matter how many times I would say, "But Tabby, you're blowing zillions of calories on the whole thing anyway, what difference can coffee ice cream possibly make?'' she'd always just shake her head and stick her nose in the air and sniff at me, then say primly to the waitress, ''Make *mine* with coffee, please.'' And as we ate our hot-fudge sundaes in the little diner, we might talk about anything: not just boys we were interested in, like everybody does, like Dorothy Fiori and my mother still, in their way, do (only the boys now are their husbands), but reincarnation, rock and roll, who her real parents might be (she was adopted), Trudy Jurgen (a Scandinavian teacher at Lakeland, an older woman we referred to as the Withered Ice Queen) and Trudy's class on comparative religion, a class we both agreed was the best thing Lakeland had going for it outside of, arguably, Paul Viguerie, a good-looking senior Tabby had a mad crush on. On the way back to Lakeland, crunching down on the crusted snow along the road, sticking our thumbs out whenever a car passed going our way, we'd sometimes sing together, harmonizing at points. She had lived part of her life in New York; she too had listened to Murray the K, and we used to harmonize on the latter part of the Murray the K jingle. ''It's Murray the K, with the swinging soirée, to play red, hot, blue-all-the-way.'' On ''red, hot, blue-all-the-way,'' she'd go up and I'd go down, and we'd giggle madly, our cheeks bright red with cold, and sing it again and again, all the way back to school, intertwined with more serious topics of discussion.

Those days were before Tab and I each went crazy—separately, the only way you can go crazy. I mean bad-crazy, of course, not having-fun-fooling-around-crazy, which we had done plenty of earlier. In those earlier days, the days when we used to escape Lakeland and sing the swinging soirée song, it would have been impossible for either of us to imagine losing each other, a process which is still going on even though I don't want it to, and am willing and able and ready to fight back. But Tabitha isn't. Can't. Walking the road to Stockbridge or Lenox in those days, singing, eating candy, our breath pluming in that cold air and both our noses bright red, wrapped in scarves and sweaters (often each others'; we swapped and borrowed clothing constantly), we couldn't have guessed what would happen to us. I suppose no one can. Sometimes it seems to me everybody, each person, is so heartbreakingly brave, just marching ahead into the future without having the faintest, slightest idea of what could be waiting for them there; sometimes when I think that, my eyes start to fill, looking at someone on the bus or train, imagining about their life. My Uncle Jay, when he showed up in his tuxedo with the white carnation to take Aunt Pat dancing ("And, oh, she was luminous, just a luminous beauty," says Katherine), could he have guessed that someday he would weep for Arkansas Black Twig apples?

Yet there are plenty of Sid Meyerhoffs who talk about "coping mechanisms" and "authenticating experiences" who certainly don't feel as I do. There are those shrinks I saw at Hurstview, and there's that Dr. Phipps, the one I saw that time when I got suspended from Lakeland. They actually manage to ignore things like mystery, fate, destiny, tragedy. They do! They seem to genuinely *believe* they can boil the whole thing up with their neat little terms. They don't know about how brave ordinary people are; they won't accept that there are things that don't fit into their little tiny tightly lidded pots, like the Holocaust or slavery or anything strong or mysterious. They don't know the first thing about Tabby and me, for instance, and what happened between us, or my parents' relationship—that people can truly *want* something to work out and the reason it doesn't is it *can't,* due to circumstances beyond anyone's control and despite the very best efforts of everyone involved.

Between hitchhiking to Lenox and now, so much has happened to Tabby and me, separately. So many bad, hard times for her and for me; and yet I did end up on the vitamins, and I guess it is not overstating it to say that they gave me back my life, or at least the possibility of it. And now I come to New York every day to attend MABEE. Lakeland and Hurstview and Grace Memorial and all those shrinks and the voices and the iron-tasting food behind me.

But for Tabby, what will come next?

She's still in Twelvetrees, she's been there since two weeks after she got expelled, which was two weeks after I got expelled, from Lakeland. She's still there. She's still locked up. She's still somewhere that she can't leave, where she can't hitchhike or take the subway or climb on a bus or hail a cab; can't go to Stockbridge or Lenox or Grand Central or Chilton or anywhere except up or down a floor to go to recreational therapy or art therapy, if they even have those things at Twelvetrees. She's still locked in and locked out, the keys in other people's hands, people that don't see her as Tabby but as a patient, an emotionally disturbed adolescent girl, very pretty, isn't it a shame, such a pretty girl, time for your medication, dear, now be a *good* girl.

She doesn't know I'm with her, for her. When you're in one of those places—I don't mean just the outside place, the mental hospital they have you incarcerated in, but the inner one, which is wide open yet totally confined and worse even than the locked ward, the locked room, the condescending doctor, the drugs—when you're there, you don't know, don't believe, can't feel, can't imagine, that *anyone* is with you or has the faintest idea of what you feel. And maybe they don't.

But they can love you. And they can want to be with and for you.

Her letters don't sound like Tab anymore.

At Hurstview they kept me so doped up I don't remember it too much; but at Grace, they took me off the Thorazine or Valium or whatever they had had me on, and I went on vitamins, and so I remember it all. There was only one exit from the ward, this thick white locked door with one tiny window of glass at eye level. It was made out of the kind of glass with wire mesh embedded in it. It looked out onto a small, windowless hall, where the elevators opened. I spent a lot of time looking at those elevators. I knew I would remember them, and the white door, and the glass with the mesh in it, forever.

Twelvetrees, where Tabitha is, is near Boston, where her adoptive parents live. Tabby doesn't know who her real parents are. It bothers her. But it bothers her adoptive parents that she wants to know; they are hurt, they ask her why she wants to know, they say, "Haven't *we* actually *been* your parents? What have we done wrong? Your biological mother just gave birth to you, we're the ones who parented you." So eventually Tabby (who once said to me, "I don't know when 'to parent' became a verb, but it just irritates the hell out of me,") just quit asking. She's been in Twelvetrees about eleven months now. I think her parents ought to tell her, if they know, about her real parents. Not that I think that's why she's flipping out; I just think it would be good if they did. Kind of . . . *polite*, in a way, though I can't say why. Not that I know why she's flipping out, though I personally believe the vitamins would help her, too. Not solve, not cure, just help. As they did me.

But, at the same time, how much can anyone *be* helped, by anything? That's what I question. I mean, so what if I don't hear voices anymore? It's like the circles;

even if you solve one there are still all those other millions of rings to deal with. Even if you get your family straightened out, there's still nuclear war.

Truthfully, I don't know anybody who's in such hot shape. There are a lot of self-congratulatory types around who *think* they are, like Jonathan, like Sid Meyerhoff who founded MABEE and who is a complete and total jerk (and someday I may tell him so, as soon as I figure out someplace else I can be besides MABEE).

But that's in the future. The present is getting home on the train through the cold, gray November dusk. The present is standing beside the track with Jonathan. He strokes my hair with one hand and nuzzles my neck with his warm, gap-toothed mouth.

"You know," he says softly, "I'm very, very good at ravishing, Elizabeth. I can make you feel very, very good. *Rilly* good."

"I'm sure you can," I say, and to my surprise I think, yeah, I bet he can. To my annoyance—since I really don't care for him—kissing him turns me on. Nothing, nothing is simple. "I'm sure you're a good lover, Jonathan. . . ."

"Oh, good doesn't begin to describe it," he says airily, dropping the hand that's been stroking my hair down to the small of my back, where it rests lightly, sending out little sparks of heat. Where did he get this confidence?

"But I'm not interested," I say firmly. "Not . . . interested. Not . . . now. Really, Jon, I'm not." Can he tell I'm lying, at least partly?

"My parents aren't at home," he wheedles. "Only the maid, and she doesn't care what I do."

In a sentence, he goes from debonair seducer to horny teenager, for which I am very thankful; it helps break the sexual thrall I might otherwise give in to. Despite myself. I don't feel like explaining to Jonathan that he just blew it for himself, or that parents are the least of my concerns. If I wanted to, he could spend the night with me at my mother's house. I've often heard her say, to Dorothy Fiori and to some of her other friends, "I figure, Elizabeth is going to do what she wants to do, so the only difference between letting her do it here versus my forbidding it and thus forcing her to go do it elsewhere, is that this way I know she's safe." "You know, Kath, I never really *thought* of it that way," says Dorothy, "but it's perfectly true. Kath, you're so smart." "Nonsense," Katherine tells her. "It's just common sense. And I just want to be sure, very sure, that Elizabeth is safe."

But after all she's been through, can she truly believe that anyone can be sure anyone else is safe?

I say to Jonathan, "Look, maybe sometime, but not now, okay? I'm tired. I'm just not up for it, okay? See you tomorrow?"

"I guess. Okay." He looks as pouty as he did in the yogurt store. He marches off.

Why do I feel older than almost everybody I know?

I get on the train to go back to Chilton. I am still extremely cold.

Three

Fly Away Home

THE NEXT DAY I shake Jonathan after school and go up alone to the Museum of Modern Art. I spend a long time in one room looking at some paintings that, I decide, are landscapes in hell. Weeping mothers are holding maimed or decapitated infants, men at war are disemboweling each other. The ground is slick with blood and pulled-out intestines, everything in deep reds and browns yet with a strange, orangy glow, as if lit by distant fires, the fires, perhaps, of these mutilated people's homes burning.

Ladybug, ladybug, fly away home. . . .

I ask myself why I'm continuing to look at these hideous paintings. I tell myself I ought to leave, I don't need these images in my head. But I stay. I keep looking.

Your house is on fire, your children will burn.

After I've walked around the room and looked at each painting, I sit on one of the padded black-leather benches and stare at one canvas in particular. They're all very similar, but maybe if I give one some time I'll be able to understand why I can't leave, why the artist made these.

The artist is German, I read that on the card accompanying the paintings. From the dates, I figure out that he painted these pictures before World War II. I try to guess about him. I don't know much about World War I, but maybe he did. Maybe he lived through it, saw the horror of war firsthand. Maybe then he *had* to paint the pictures because, horrible though they were, they were the strongest thing he had ever seen in his life and the images just stayed inside him until he put them down on canvas and he was free of them then. Or maybe he never got free of them—maybe he became a pacifist and a peace activist and these paintings were done as propaganda, to convince people, to show them, how terrible war is.

Or maybe he *liked* war, whether or not he was actually in the first one. Or maybe he saw, he sensed, what was coming; maybe he was either politically astute or psychic, precognitive. Or maybe he just saw something in the Germans (and in himself?), a potential for violence, and he painted it, and it was the same thing that came out later in what the Nazis did to Jews not that long afterward.

In Chilton, though we're a mile from the station, the freight trains that go by at night can easily be heard. They have a different sound than the commuter trains—a long, slow, drawn-out clackety-clackety, more gentle but louder than the day trains, and they have a high, long, lonely whistle. When I'm lying awake in bed sometimes, my mother already asleep, my father downstairs listening to jazz very softly on the stereo, smoking cigarettes, reading, every so often getting up to walk heavily to the pantry underneath my bedroom to pull on the light, slide out a bottle, pour another drink, slide the bottle back, pull out the light, all the time alone, completely unaware that I too am awake, alone, upstairs: when, at these times, I hear the freight trains, I feel lonely and afraid. I always think about the Nazis taking the Jews away in freight trains, which leads me to other injustices, like black people being lynched in the South, like slavery in the first place, like Russian dissidents being jailed in mental hospitals and given drugs to silence their protests and being called insane—things so bad I know I can never imagine how bad they really were or are, no matter how much I think about them; but also things I can't do anything about, and I feel guilty for my own unhappiness. Knowing how much other people have suffered, in such monstrous ways, I ought to be happier.

I straighten my back in the museum. The black padded benches are backless. I have lousy posture unless I work on it.

My family is Jewish, though you would never know it by our behavior. I have never in my life been in a synagogue. Passover and Yom Kippur are just names of holidays; I have no idea what they mean or how they're celebrated. I don't even know what Jews aren't supposed to eat besides pork. At the house in Chilton, we always have a tree at Christmas, without any religious significance. I have been in a Christian church, though, once. My mother says that when I was little, Jay-Lynne, the baby-sitter, took me with her to the Catholic church in Chilton.

"You were so cute about it when you came home, those big blue eyes of yours opened up wide with excitement—you looked enchanting! I asked you, 'What was it like?' and you said ecstatically, 'Jay-Lynne goes to church and lights candles and sings happy birthday to you!' "

My mother loves to tell stories about me as a child. She also tells about how, when the house was being repainted, I leaned out a second-floor window and called up to the workmen, "Painters, please give us a nice polka-dot trim."

I think it was easier for my mother when I was little than now.

Now you *would* know we're Jewish as far as our looks go, at least my father and I (my mother and Aunt Pat are both very Waspy in appearance). My father and I have dark hair and giant, classic noses, though our eyes are blue, not brown. Still, we look like people in concentration-camp pictures, the new arrivals when they were first allowed off the trains, when they were still fleshed out and their hair had not yet been shaved off, before they were starved to the terrible skeletal staring thin sameness that's in the later pictures.

I sometimes stand in front of the mirror and cover part of my nose with my hand and imagine how I'd look with a smaller nose. Much prettier, I think. Once, my first year at Lakeland, a senior named Jane Alexander said to me, "You know, Elizabeth, I don't want you to take this wrong, but I have to tell you—you'd be *soooo* beautiful if you got a nose job."

I later told my mother this story, when I was home on Easter break that year, told her simply as something that had happened to me, like I would say, "Did you hear what happened to the girl who fell into the lens-grinding machine?" and she'd say, "No, what?" and I'd say, "She made a spectacle out of herself," and my mother would groan and laugh. I save jokes for my mother, any joke I hear, no matter how stupid it is; and I save any absurd or strange or funny thing that happens to me, save it to tell her, because usually she'll laugh.

Most of the time she is so sad that I love to make her laugh when I can.

But instead of being amused at this funny thing Jane Alexander said to me, rude, outrageous (Tabby had said, "I've always thought Jane Alexander could use a brain job, myself"), my mother was furious. "Oh, that is so *untrue,* honey! You are absolutely beautiful the way you are, and you always have been! The nerve of that girl!"

My mother *believes* this, too, that I'm gorgeous. Not in the way that *I* think, every so often, that I'm attractive, which is in a very unusual, exotic, offbeat, strong kind of way that has to do more with the way I think than how I look and has nothing to do with any prettiness or beauty you'd ever see on a model. No. My mother thinks I'm classically, for-real beautiful. Though I have a big nose in a world where small noses are the preferred way to go; though I have frizzy-curly light-brown short hair in a world where blond hair, shoulder length or longer, wavy or straight but not frizzy-curly, is the preferred hair; though I am a little too big, both big-boned big and ten-to-fifteen pounds big, my mother genuinely, firmly believes that I am a classic beauty.

I have pointed out to her, for as long as I can remember, that since she's my mother she just *might* be prejudiced in my favor. She will never concede on this point.

"That's ridiculous! My being your mother has *nothing* whatso*ever* to do with my being able to perceive beauty! And remember, Elizabeth, my entire professional life is based on perceptions of beauty and talent and . . . and . . . style! And you have all three, and your being my daughter has *nothing* to do with my being able to recognize it!"

She is vehement on the subject.

The night after I told her about Jane Alexander's comment, she knocked on my door.

"Elizabeth?" Hesitatingly.

I was on my bed, reading. "Come on in," I said. I put my book down; it was *Demian,* by Hermann Hesse.

She pushed open the door and stood there for a minute in her full-length turquoise blue bathrobe. She rarely wears any makeup, so Katherine's face doesn't look much different in the evening from how it looks when she first gets up or in the daytime. But just before she goes to sleep she puts on moisturizer, which leaves her skin slightly shiny. Her face had that after-moisturizer sheen to it, and when she came over and sat at my desk I could smell from my bed its distinctive scent, a sweet, clean, slightly medicinal but not unpleasant fragrance, like a mixture of fresh apples and air-conditioned pharmacies.

"Well, I've been thinking all day about what that awful girl said to you." She sighed and looked away from me a moment, then back to me. "I know you've never believed me all these years when I've told you you're beautiful. But you are, you are, you are. However . . ." She paused.

I waited, then prompted, "However?"

"However," she said, "I've been thinking that if your nose really bothers you, then maybe we should do something about it. Not because I think you need it, not because I think it could in any way improve your attractiveness, but because, if it causes you unhappiness, it can be changed. If you'd feel better about yourself with a different nose, well then, we could arrange to have it changed, if we don't go to New England this summer."

God, why did I tell her?

"Look, really, it doesn't bother me that much, Katherine. I was just telling you what Jane Alexander said because it seemed funny to me. No big deal." It's complicated, how I look, how I feel about how I look; how the Nazis killed Jews, why I can't or won't change the tiny bit of me that is Jewish even though I don't like the way it looks; how the idea of plastic surgery is both repellent to me (because it's totally artificial and dishonest) and seductive (because imagine being able just simply to revise yourself, edit out what is ugly or out of place and make it beautiful and alluring or in fashion or at least nondescript). And over and above all that, it just seems wrong to me that doctors spend their time, and patients their money, revising faces when every day in the paper there are stories of South American children going blind from easily preventable diseases and pictures of African women with distended bellies holding tiny skeletal children. Not that my having or not having a nose job would affect any of these in the least.

But I can't begin to talk about this with Katherine, with anyone. Too complicated. As usual, I am thinking too much.

I repeated, "No, I just thought it was kind of funny."

"Funny!" Katherine snorted. "Funny! Well! The depths of that kind of extreme rudeness . . . But never mind. I'm just glad, so glad and relieved, that you don't want to do it. Because truly, Elizabeth, *honestly,* whether you believe me or not, you are such a lovely girl and it would be a shame, worse than a shame, a travesty almost, to alter your face." She looked at me, sighed, shook her head. She stood up, came over to the bed, took my hand and squeezed it, looking down at me. I smelled the faint apple smell.

"I just didn't want you to be unhappy," she said.

But nobody can save anybody else from unhappiness. Sometimes it seems to me that's all my mother has ever wanted: for me not to be unhappy. I have let her down.

When I hear about parents like Cam Peckinpaker's, I

know, I know, I know how lucky I am to have a mother like Katherine. I love her. Yes. I do.

But I wish she would worry more about her own happiness and let me worry about mine.

As it is, I fail her.

As it is, I worry about *her* and feel helpless.

I wish she would write her novel. I wish she would leave Rahleigh and Byrd if she hates it so much. But does she? Can she? If I hated someplace as much as she seems to hate Rahleigh, I'd leave it . . . as I'm planning to leave MABEE as soon as I can figure out some other place to be.

But if she does hate it, how can she glow when she talks about, for instance, discovering Edmund Weller? I know her, she can't fool me; I know when she's faking it to be politic. I know she is still genuinely thrilled over Edmund and his small children at play with their giant beach balls, and some of the others. Besides, she couldn't be so good at it, could she, if she hated it?

Then there's the divorce. "*That* whole can of worms," as Dorothy Fiori likes to say of any messy or painful topic.

Katherine is the one that wanted the divorce. She asked my father, not the other way around. Their marriage was never happy, though passionate, and it had its moments (mostly when they were discussing books and authors or plays or art or movies, never when they talked, or tried to, about themselves). "It had to end," she has said. That is the closest she can come to saying she ended it. She always implies that my father left her, which he didn't. Well, he did and he didn't. He left at one point; she kicked him out at another. But the divorce, this, definitely, is something she is seeking and he is not.

Though that fact, unadmitted, has not made her sigh

any less. Does it make any difference about who left whom?

It would to me. I would a thousand times over rather leave than be left.

I think about Katherine's sighs. The coming-home-on-the-train-drink-of-bourbon sighs; or when I say, "How was your day?" and she says, "Oh," and here is where she sighs, "Oh, my day, it's too much, I don't want to go into it; how was yours?"

Then there are all the sighs connected with Walter and their past. Things that happened a good—let me count, well, Steph is twenty-four now, and she goes back, in remembering some of the things, to way before he was born—things that happened twenty or even thirty years ago, still cause her to sigh.

"I remember how, when we married, it was to be a marriage of equals, Elizabeth," she says, with what I know is the first of many sighs that will accompany this story, that accompany the many similar stories she tells me. Just when I think she'd told me all of them (and she does repeat them) she'll throw in a new one. "It was going to be a marriage of passion and intellect." She sighs again, and then begins in earnest.

"We were living in the Village when I was pregnant with Steph, and every Saturday night we used to go out with this group of people, friends of Walter's and mine—it changed from week to week depending on who was in town, but always it was bright, funny, interesting, stimulating people. Poets, actors, a professor from the drama department at Columbia . . . well. We'd go out Saturdays and eat somewhere where the food wasn't much, but that wasn't what you were there for. You were there for the discussions, the camaraderie. Sometimes, then, we'd go out together to hear jazz, but mostly we'd just go on to someone's apartment or to a café and drink wine, and sometimes go out later for coffee and pastry. Occasionally we'd hear someone lecture, or give a poetry reading. I remember . . . well. Anyway, after Steph was born, he and I were both home from the hospital and Saturday rolled around, the first Saturday since I'd had the baby. And Walter just looked at me around eight o'clock and said, 'Bye, see you later.' And he was gone, like that. No discussion, no anything.'' She sighs. ''So much for equality, for a passionate meeting of minds and hearts.''

''But why didn't you just get a baby-sitter?''

''Honey, we couldn't afford it. Besides, Steph was too young to be left with a baby-sitter.''

''Well, why didn't you try to talk about it with Walter? Why didn't you say, 'This isn't fair, this isn't right, this isn't what we agreed on?' ''

''Honey,'' says my mother, sighing again, ''it was a whole different day, a whole different time. Women didn't . . . well, you weren't there, you can't imagine.''

Why does she bother telling me, if she doesn't think I can imagine?

What does it matter, anyway, what women in general did? She and Walter ran with a bohemian set; she could have done something if she wanted to, I'm sure. Probably people would have even respected her for it, probably the other women would have said ''Bravo!''

But, of course, I *wasn't* there. It's so irritating; it's like people saying, ''When you're my age you'll understand.'' There's no real answer to that. If you say, ''Well, no matter what age I am, no matter what era it is, I might just do it differently than you do it''—or did it, in Katherine's case—they can still say, ''But you weren't there, and you're seventeen years old, and you've never done what I've done and felt what I felt so you can't possibly know what I'd do." And there's no answer.

"You weren't there," or "You'll understand when you're my age," finish it as a discussion. Suddenly, I am listening to my mother tell me about bad things that happened to her. How am I supposed to participate?

"Besides," adds my mother, "*life* isn't fair."

The Nazis took the nonpracticing, nonbelieving Jews away with the religious ones. They would take me just as quickly as they would take those weird-looking, pale Hasidic Jews with the beards and the long curly side-burns. They would take away my Wasp-looking, soft-spoken mother; certainly they would take away my loud, funny, screwed-up Jewish-looking father.

"Pretty grotesque, aren't they?"

A man sits down on the bench next to me at the Museum. He wears glasses, a corduroy jacket with patches on the elbows, no tie. Twenty-five, twenty-six. He has a lumpy though pleasant face that reminds me of mashed potatoes.

"But absorbing," I reply. This, apparently, is my day for a meet-cute.

"Yes, *you* were certainly absorbed in them," he says. "You didn't even notice me. I've been looking at you for at least ten minutes."

I know a pickup when I hear one; but so what, I'm not doing anything else. "Most people," I say to him, "come here to look at the pictures."

He smiles faintly but doesn't reply. Instead he asks, "Well, what were you thinking about them?"

"About the paintings?" I nod toward the dismembered babies.

"Umm-hmm."

I notice that the cuff of his striped oxford shirt, protruding from the sleeve of his jacket, is frayed. A few threads drift on his bony wrist. "I was thinking what an excellent grip on reality that artist had."

I wasn't thinking this at all, but it's what comes out when I open my mouth. It certainly sounds impressively cynical.

He eyes me uneasily until he decides I'm joking, then laughs. "Well, aren't *you* something," he says. (Sure, who isn't?) "Are you an artist?"

I shake my head.

"You look like an artist."

I shrug. I'm wearing jeans tucked into shiny cobalt blue rubber boots, a big checked shirt with a high collar, a green turtleneck underneath. My down jacket, gray on one side and reversible to blue on the other, is lying across my lap, both its colors visible. "What does an artist look like?" I ask him.

"Oh, I don't know," he says sheepishly. He pauses, then makes a recovery with, "But what *do* you do, then, if you're not an artist?"

"I'm a writer. Would-be. Unpublished." In one sentence I have already told this stranger, who has greasy light brown hair, more than I've told Jonathan in a month and a half. Revelation is something to spread around.

"Well, a writer is an artist, in a generic sense."

Generic artist. I see myself in black pants, white shirt, a broad-brimmed black hat that dips down over one eye. Simple, unembellished, like the generic chocolate pudding or tomato paste at the A&P where my mother and I shop on Saturdays with Dorothy Fiori.

I shrug again. My all-purpose, generic response.

"What do you do meanwhile?" he asks.

"Meanwhile?"

"Meanwhile till you get published."

"Kill time. Frequent museums." I don't tell him that I'm seventeen, have been in two mental hospitals and was once diagnosed as a suicidal paranoid-schizophrenic but was saved by a controversial therapy, vitamin megadoses, that almost nobody believes in. All of which killed a great deal of time, and almost killed me. I don't tell him this and I don't tell him a lot more. He obviously thinks I'm older and more together than I am. People often make this mistake, especially male people.

"Well," he says, "I teach." Though I haven't asked him, he adds, "History, at Walden School."

I suppress a smile. Walden is a private school in New York for bright, overprivileged kids like me. They turned me down because of my brilliant record of craziness.

"I've heard of it," I say.

"Hal Gillette," he says suddenly, sticking out his hand. I'm supposed to take this hand with one of my hands. Shake it. Tell him my name. I wait a fraction of a second before I do this. His hand is cool and slightly, unpleasantly moist, much larger than mine. I have tiny hands: long fingers, but tiny hands. Pretty. Maybe my best feature.

"Tell you what, Elizabeth, let me buy you a cup of coffee," says Hal Gillette, with an odd brightness, as if this were a startlingly original idea.

Why not? What else am I doing?

I lied when I told my mother my nose doesn't bother me. It does. I know very well I'm not beautiful in the regular kind of cheerleadery, shampoo-or-makeup-ad, model way. And of course I would like to be (though if I felt the same inside it wouldn't do me much good—but surely I wouldn't feel the same if I was that kind of beautiful).

Now Tabitha, my old friend from Lakeland, *she* was beautiful.

Not that it solved any problems for her.

I know having my nose chopped off wouldn't be enough to make me beautiful, but it would be a step in that direction.

But it would be *wrong*. It would be going with the Nazis, cooperating with them. It would also be going along with the cheerleaders, the people who write the makeup and shampoo ads, the editors of magazines who pick and discard and shape what all of us, or most of us, or at least I, think is beautiful. The people who told me that what I was wasn't beautiful. They did a good enough job so I believe them—but not so good a job that I think I *should* believe them, that I think it's *right* that I believe them. If you know you're brainwashed, are you still brainwashed?

Tabby said once, "When we're both forty-five, you know what people are going to say? 'Ah, that Elizabeth Stein, such an interesting woman, such a fascinating face.' But me, it'll be, 'Ah that Tabitha Whittaker, great pity, used to be such a great beauty.' " Tabby thinks I'm lucky, or used to, because I know what I want to do, to write, and she doesn't have any idea and is afraid she will just drift or get married "or otherwise lead a dull and boring meaningless life."

And many, many times she said, with a vague wave of her hands, usually after someone had complimented her, of her beauty, "It's all just outside, outside stuff."

So, I turned my mother down because I didn't want to cooperate with the Nazis, couldn't be artificial, couldn't stand to get the kind of face I wanted, because I hate wanting it.

She was glad I turned her down, but she doesn't understand fully why I did. How could she? I didn't even try to explain it to her, though I know she'd agree completely. I've heard her put down "self-created Hollywood phonies,'' some of them people my father writes about. ''Not even *self*-created in some cases; it's all done by the press agent, the director, the makeup man. . . .'' Oh, she'd get what I'm saying, she's not an artificial person. She would probably even understand about the Nazis, even though that is hard to explain. Anything I tried to put into words she would honestly try to understand—maybe even try too hard, which is one reason, perhaps, I keep things from her.

Katherine's problem, one of them at least, is she loves me too much and it keeps her from doing what she wants to do. (But hasn't she always, to hear her tell me about her life, not done what she wants to do, long before I was even there for her not to do it for?) I know her love for me keeps her from things, her past notwithstanding; it must, though she would probably deny it because she wouldn't want to make me feel guilty (though she does, anyway, most of the time).

For though Katherine is not artificial or phony, she is often dishonest for reasons of ''tact and grace'' as she puts it, though talking kindly to Cam Peckinpaker while she makes faces of despair and disgust at me is not my idea of either. I personally think it would do Cam Peckinpaker a lot of good to be told off once by mother. ''Look, Cam, it's Sunday, give me a break. I'm with my family. I need a little breathing room. I'm just getting a divorce; surely you can wait out one weekend without my telling you how to get through it.''

Telling Cam Peckinpaker off, though, goes in the snowball-in-hell file.

My mother doesn't want to hurt anyone's feelings.

She doesn't look after her own feelings enough, that's what I think. That's what tangles everything up.

I can't explain why, but I *know* her not looking after

her own feelings hurts mine. I don't get why this should be, but it's true. I can *feel* it's true. I *almost* get it.

My mother is always eager to know anything about me. She questions me with eagerness and hunger (not suspicion). What am I reading? Oh, *that*. What do I think of that author? Where did I have lunch today, what did I have; oh, was it good? What am I wearing, what am I thinking, whom did I meet, what did we talk about?

It is this eagerness that makes me not tell her things, often, though I feel I am depriving her. But I want to, I have to, keep something back for myself. Though I have no idea of what "myself" is, it makes me uneasy to feel so much of Katherine is riding on it. I am on a fragile, spun-glass foundation, easily shattered. Her happiness shouldn't depend on mine, for mine is nonexistent.

It's funny about boys, or even men, like Hal Gillette, who is now vigorously forking into a strawberry tart, shiny as if it had been lacquered, as we drink coffee looking out into the sculpture garden. It is raining hard and will probably turn into sleet, then snow; and if it snows enough it will disguise the city and everything will look pretty, pure, as if it hadn't yet been born or made mistakes.

"A lot of them are spoiled," says Hal Gillette. "Spoiled *rotten*. Just obnoxious. They look down on me, of course." There are pastry crumbs on his lapel. "They tell me about their skiing trips in Gstaad over winter break; the poor ones have to go to Colorado. On what Walden pays me, believe me, I couldn't take a trip to Hoboken to play pool."

Hal Gillette, like Jonathan, like Harvey whom I was seeing a lot of before I went into the mental hospital and whom I kind of liked; like Jack, my speed-freak boyfriend at Grace Memorial; like Gary Shields, who was the first person I ever slept with back at Lakeland, in the gymnasium on the wrestling mat; like men I've just talked to, for instance when Tabby and I used to pick up men in Provincetown, the summer between our freshman and sophomore years at Lakeland—they're all so easy to talk to, you never have to say anything.

Before I went to Lakeland, which was coed, I was scared of boys, shy because I'm not pretty in a conventional way (but I won't go into all that again), and because I really didn't *know* any boys, not just to sit around and talk with. My brother, Steph, is nine years older than me; he left home the year I was eight.

But quickly I found out you don't have to say much with boys, just listen and kind of go along, and if you hold something back (and I do), it just enthralls them.

"All the same," says Hal Gillette, "I like teaching; I like kids. And history—the way I feel is, learning about the past is the only real insurance there is for the future."

I'll think about that one, understanding the past to insure the future, but offhand it seems to me unlikely, maybe impossible, to do either. But not now. I don't want to think about anything. I want to drift, not really hearing but listening to the sound of his voice, sipping the warm coffee, gazing out into the rainy sculpture garden, occasionally looking directly at Hal. Dreamily I decide he has a weak chin. I decide he'd look better with a mustache. A beard might help, too. He blots his lips on a napkin.

"Besides, I like teaching itself, the process," says Hal Gillette. "I like the moment something gets through and you know you really opened their vision, even if only for a moment."

I don't know exactly what I mean by "hold something back," except that I do it. I don't know what the "something" is: It's not sex—I've had sex pretty often, and I still hold back the "something," whatever it is. It's some part of me that's a mystery, maybe even to me; but boys and men can tell they don't possess it or haven't been shown it, whatever it is, and that I'm not going to show it to them. This seems to draw them like ants to Coke spilled on a sidewalk in the summer. I feel it may be my essence or what I am deep down under all the layers. But if I don't know what that is, how can I give it or share it with someone even if I wanted to? And I'm not sure if I *do* want to. Maybe I do want to, long to, even, but I'm not sure.

And in a different way, I hold back with my parents. I hold back with my mother, who wants to know everything about me, and with my father, who wants to know nothing.

I got into the holding-back habit early. It's like hiding something for safekeeping, except then you forget where you put it.

Sometimes I can almost remember, the way you can almost but not quite remember a dream sometimes, a time when I didn't hold back at all. An enthusiasm, a complete openness and curiosity—I had this as a very young child; maybe all children do. I remember my favorite color was red. I remember I liked dresses with full skirts and pockets. I remember when we drove into New York from Chilton along the Saw Mill River Parkway that I leaned out the window to ask the toll takers, "What's your name?" and that most of them told me; and that one of them, a man named Bill, remembered me and used to ask me, when we stopped at his tollbooth, "How's my little cupcake today?" And I can't remember, but I can easily imagine, asking the painters to give us a polka-dot trim. What happened to all that? Is it still inside me somewhere? Is it still inside everybody? Is it because it's so sad to lose that that everybody has amnesia about being a young child?

I would never wear bright red now. I wear gray, black, brown, navy blue. The brightest I go is cobalt blue, like the shiny rubber rain boots I have on today.

Ladybug, ladybug—who wrote that ominous children's rhyme anyway? Where did I learn it?

Girls are much harder to be with. You can't win them with nothing-talk. It takes effort—which is why I know many more male people than female, though I'm not actually close to them; I just spend time with them (like this second with Hal Gillette) and sometimes have sex with them.

Tabby and I were friends to the point where we *almost* didn't hold back. Maybe we still are friends, though each letter from her, from Twelvetrees, sounds stranger and weaker, like a signal fading on the radio, like when late at night, from Provincetown, we tried to pick up Murray the K from New York. Very, very occasionally we succeeded, whereupon we squealed with excitement (and once Tabby remarked happily, throwing her head back, "Oh, we're *such* typical teenagers!"). But now Tabby's fading, blips of interference, and even though I fiddle with the tuner button I can't seem to get her back.

And I miss her.

I continue looking out into the Museum of Modern Art sculpture garden. Hal Gillette is still talking, and I have been making noncommittal "umm-hmm" answers. A large gray granite female nude is just on the other side of the glass, out in that pouring rain. I wonder why fat looks so good in sculpture and paintings and so lousy in person—in the flesh, as it were—and in photographs. Maybe, again, this is more magazine brainwashing.

"Do you have a car, Elizabeth?"

I tune in. *"What?"* No one in New York drives; this is startling. The rain slants into the sculpture garden. Once, when I was little, my father took me to a jazz concert here, a black flutist he'd written an article about. The high, sweet clean notes fell from the silver flute like water trickling down, falling from a high place. My father and I sat on the ground and the end of his cigarette glowed in the semidark of that summer night. Afterward he took me up to meet the musician, who squatted down on the ground so we were eye to eye and put his hands on my shoulders. He gave me a dazzlingly warm and genuine smile and said, "Hey, how you doin', Elizabeth?" Yes, I know he had to be kind because I was the daughter of a man who had just given his career a boost. And I know, too, the flutist was still excited from having given such a good performance. But there was more. That musician emanated something. A boundless energetic satisfaction, a connection with life itself, a connection—for that moment—with me, a small white girl in red overalls. I just looked at him, enchanted, wordless, and then I put my arms around his neck. He lifted me up, hugged me and handed me back to my father, both of them laughing, and my father hugged me. On the drive home, my eyes half closed, I thought about that music like a waterfall, the musician's smile, those white, white teeth in that dusky, handsome face under the dark summer sky, being hugged, handed over, hugged again, from one tall grown man to another.

I wonder if my father remembers that evening. I miss my father now. I think I always have, though.

"A card, a card! A business card, with your number on it!" Hal Gillette is agitated.

"Oh! No, no, I don't."

"Well, here, then write on this." He pushes a paper

napkin toward me, a clean one, pulls a black ballpoint pen from his jacket pocket, clicks it open, lays it across the napkin: an invitation. Do I wish to attend? As if I am as unformed as the smoke from one of my father's cigarettes drifting into the heavy moist air I wonder, *Why is Hal Gillette so urgent?* Are he and Jonathan so desperate for just a few umm-hmms and a roll in the hay? How can they *care* so much about nothing nothing nothing at all?

And who is the prophet singing to the ladybug about her doomed children? Singing, although it is too late?

"I don't give my number out," I tell Hal Gillette. "I hope you understand. New York. . . ."

"Oh, yeah, sure." He looks crushed. Picks up the pen, clicks the point back in, replaces it in his pocket. "Well, at least take mine, then, would you?" He's already digging out a business card, curved in the shape of his wallet which is curved in the shape of his butt.

"Sure," I say, taking the curved business card. His face lights up.

"I can understand why you wouldn't want to give out your phone number," he says, quickly, eagerly, "but please, please, do feel free to call me. I mean it! I'm not one of these guys who think women shouldn't call men. Hell, no! Takes the pressure off us! Hey, I think it's great!"

"Sure," I say. "Maybe I will." I look at my watch. Four twenty-nine; if I hurry I can catch the four fifty-five to Chilton. Fly away home. I look up to see that Hal Gillette has seen me looking at my watch; he's crestfallen. I add, "Look, in case I lose or misplace this, is your number listed?"

"Umm-hmm," he says. "But don't lose it."

On the way to the train I drop Hal Gillette's card in a trash basket.

Four

Just a Few Inches of Flesh

"LOOK, my aunt's husband of thirty-five years just died two and a half weeks ago. I need to go visit her. It's not the kind of thing you can come along on!"

Jonathan sulks, staring out the window of the MABEE common room at the gray slanting rain. We both have a free period. Usually on free period I go out and walk around, but it's so miserable today that I'm staying inside. I have a copy of Christopher Isherwood's *The Berlin Stories,* which I was intending to read, having forgotten that Jon also has free period at this time today and would insist on my paying attention to him. I glance longingly at my book on the coffee table, closed, unread.

MABEE occupies one floor of a small, overheated building near Gramercy Park. After I leave here this afternoon I'm going to visit my aunt, meet my father for dinner, then go with him to a party at his new girlfriend's house.

The windows at the end of the common room face onto the backs of other buildings. I know that from where Jonathan is sitting he can see down to the ground, trashy back lots. He remains obstinately silent. I don't feel like jollying him up.

"Well, okay?" I ask him. "I'm going, I'm going alone, I have to, and that's it."

"What do you expect me to say, Elizabeth?" he snaps. "Do what you want to do; you don't need my permission."

"I *know* I don't need your permission, Jon, I haven't made any kind of commitment to you. I just want to feel like—"

"You told me you would think about it!" Jonathan looks away from the window to gaze at me furiously, then turns back to the wet glass.

"I *am* thinking about it!" "It" means sex, specifically me having it with Jonathan.

"If you'll excuse me," says Jon coldly, "*I'm* going to meditate." He walks over to the couch, takes off his shoes, and pulls his knees up into a lotus position. After shooting me a single, final, annoyed glance, he closes his eyes.

"If you'll excuse *me,"* I say, "you need it. I'm going out, swami."

Though Barnes & Noble is only one block away, I'm drenched when I get there. I shake the water off my head like a dog.

The clerk, a pleasantly nondescript young woman with shoulder-length brown hair, is sitting by the cash register. I've seen her here several times before. She puts down her book when I enter and, watching me, smiles. "Pretty wet out there," she says.

"Sure is," I reply.

I envy her her job. I would love to work in a bookstore. Someday maybe I will ask her if there are any openings.

The huge bookstore is almost empty; there seems to

be only me and the one clerk by the front door. I spend the next hour browsing. It is warm and dry there, and the heating system makes a pleasantly neutral background whooshing sound. I wander around from stack to stack. Poetry, novels, drama, anthropology, psychology, biography—each draw me. Each ask, I think, in different ways, the questions that I am asking. But possibly those authors have answers in all those millions of white pages, answers waiting to come to life as I pick up each book and take in the black words, answers that I don't have.

Then again, maybe all those authors were writing not because they had answers, but because they had questions. When I think of the authors I know personally—my father, Cam Peckinpaker, some of the others that work with Katherine or that she's told me about, even when I think of myself as a potential writer—I have to admit that this hypothesis is more credible. A potential writer; is there such a thing really, I wonder? Isn't everyone a potential writer? It's something anyone *could* do pretty easily as far as the physical skills are concerned (and to hear Katherine tell the weird stories of people who have approached her with manuscripts, like the nurse in the recovery room when she was coming out of anesthesia after she had a hysterectomy years ago, most people want to). Potential—it goes on my "to think about" list; but right now, in Barnes & Noble, I don't want to do anything but drift among the books in this neutral, warm place.

I wind up buying *In My Mother's House*, by Colette, because that is my situation and because I love Colette's writing, which always makes me think of biting into ripe fruit, like a peach so juicy you bend over so as not to spatter your shirt. I also purchase a book called *A Time to Grieve; How to Survive the Loss of a Love*. There are five whole shelves of books on death, dying, grieving, mourning, coping with the death of one's children, one's parents, one's spouse. I read the comments on the backs of many of them before I select *A Time to Grieve.* I figure maybe I'll give it to my aunt when I visit her, if it seems appropriate. If it doesn't, I can always use it. No one that I am close to has died recently, but I still spend a lot of time grieving. Some tips or suggestions might be transferable to general grief.

As I pay for my books I notice what the Barnes & Noble clerk is reading: *Tales of Power,* by Carlos Castaneda. I've always meant to read those Castaneda books. When I leave I see her pick up her book again, but as I push open the door she looks up and says, "Have a nice day."

I go back out into the rain.

Back at MABEE it is time for my next class, psychology. It is difficult for me to use a word like "class," in reference to MABEE, without putting quote marks around it or referring to it as so-called. Students, classes, teachers, principal—all these common, ordinary school words have no reference at all to what takes place at MABEE. Anyway, we so-called students pick what we want to study, and the poor souls who pass for teachers cast around among themselves for who could possibly, conceivably "teach" it. In fact, the "teachers" are all Sid Meyerhoff's patients, and MABEE his way to provide constant contact with him, their shrink. Take kids who have gotten turned away from any other kind of school that would conceivably take them, take desperate parents, preferably moneyed, and take Sid's adult patients who cannot cope with the world. Form a school. The adults teach the kids, the parents foot the bill, Sid keeps a close eye on everything, his beloved patients under his close supervision, his watchful and therapeutic eye. Sid, a beefy Weight Watchers member, is of course the "principal" of the school. The so-called school.

Every single one of Sid's adult patients is female.

Sid's office complex, which includes a kitchen, nursery, bathrooms, and a couple of secretaries' desks, is to the right when you get out of the elevator; MABEE is to the left. When I exit the elevator, sopping wet but restored by an hour at Barnes & Noble, Abby, a dark-haired woman of about thirty-five who is the one deemed most fit to teach me psychology, is waiting for me. "Sid wants to see you, Elizabeth," she says.

"Okay," I say. My wet coat drips puddles onto the floor. "Can I hang up my coat first?"

"Sure, sure," she says impatiently, already pressing buttons on a phone. "Elizabeth's on her way," she says importantly into the receiver.

I hang my coat in the common room, shake some of the water off my head, and cross to Sid's side. I do not, not, not want to be going to talk to Sidney Meyerhoff.

"He'll be with you in a second, Elizabeth," says Jean, Sid's secretary.

From the chair outside Sid's office I can distinctly hear Sid saying, "Yeah, well, of course, that's a perfect coping mechanism for her, wouldn't you say?" He pauses, then continues. "Look, Ann, the next time she won't get off the phone with you, you want to know what you say? I'll tell you what you say. You say, 'Ma, I have to go to the bathroom. Good-bye.' You do that a few times, I guarantee you, she'll get the message."

Jean, overhearing this, giggles conspiratorially. "Isn't

he *something?''* she says to me admiringly. I recall Hal Gillette asking me the same question about myself. I fervently hope that the something I am bears no resemblance to the something Sid is.

The door opens and the person Sid has been talking to comes out. It's Ann Gryschinski, who teaches me comparative religion. Again, so-called, so-called, so-called.

''Hi, Elizabeth,'' she says to me.

''Come on in, Elizabeth,'' booms Sid from within the office. ''How 'bout a warm fuzzie?''

At the end of my interview here (a formality really, they take everyone they can get), Sid said to me, ''How 'bout a warm fuzzie, Elizabeth?''

I must have looked as blank as I felt horrified, for Sid continued brightly, ''That's *our* name for a hug here at MABEE. A warm fuzzie doesn't *have* to be physical, though; it can be a verbal positive stroke as well. But when *we* say 'warm fuzzie' around *here*, we usually mean just a nice, big hug.''

I opened my mouth, but shut it again. I've been around shrinks enough to guess their style on short acquaintance. With Sid, I knew immediately protests would generate a lecture which would not conclude until I agreed with him and offered up, as proof, the requisite warm fuzzie. To save time, then, I stood and clasped him perfunctorily.

Sid looked at me, pained. ''Oh, Elizabeth,'' he said sadly. ''When we hugged just now, I noticed how you keep your distance. You just hug with your arms. *That's* not a warm fuzzie!'' He continued to survey me with pity and deep concern. ''When we hugged, Elizabeth, I noticed how you kept your vagina about ten feet away from my penis. There's nothing to be *scared* of. Not *all* good feelings of closeness are sexual; a hug often just says, 'Hello, we're both human beings and we're both okay!' It can be a good, close *human* feeling that isn't sexual at all. And not all feelings that *are* sexual are bad, anyway! Even if we sometimes have sexual feelings that *are* inappropriate, they don't need to be played out; we don't need to give in to them unless we *want* to, so those feelings need *never* threaten us!"

Thus I learned the appropriate full-body human MABEE hug. Or else. "When we're unwilling to express our natural, human feelings in a warm, natural way, like a genuine hug, Elizabeth, that shows a certain resistance, a lack of commitment to good mental health."

I walked out of Sid's office that day literally nauseated. My mother, who had already been told that MABEE would accept me if I wished, was sitting there hopefully, waiting.

Fourteen schools, including Walden, had turned me down, thanks to my mental-hospital record. Ordinary public school, of course, wouldn't touch me; I was "emotionally disturbed." My parents, though not rich like the average MABEE parents, fit the profile in the most important way: They were desperate.

I had caused them enough trouble, Katherine particularly.

My mother said, "Well, how do you like it, honey?" Her tone was so bright and hopeful.

I said, "Fine, great! I think it'll be really good here."

And I was rewarded with the rare sight of my mother smiling with profound relief.

Besides, I had to be somewhere.

But now it is four months later, a cold and rainy November afternoon, and I am walking into Sid's office as Ann is walking out. I am wishing that I were walking in for our final session, the one where I say, "Sid, I'm leaving MABEE in five minutes and I'm never coming back. You are a conning, manipulative, sick man and . . ." Well, I don't have all the details worked out yet.

But I'm not to that point yet. "I am a camera with its shutter open, quite passive, recording, not thinking," says Christopher Isherwood, describing himself as a young man in Berlin just before the Nazis came to power. "Some day, all this," he says, meaning everything he sees, "will have to be developed, carefully printed, fixed." And of course, one day it was, and that's why I have *The Berlin Stories* to read today, all these years later. Going into Sid's office I think, I am a camera, too.

I give Sid the requisite warm fuzzie. It's a bit like hugging the Pillsbury dough boy.

"So, Elizabeth," says Sid, settling himself into his giant desk chair and leaning backward into it. "What's happening? How are you feeling these days?"

"Fine," I say.

"Everything going all right?"

"Yeah, fine." I smile brightly, hiding my extreme wariness. And all the time, I think, the camera is going click, click, click. I watch myself watching myself watching myself. Like two mirrors facing each other, the images stretch into infinity. And Sid has no idea, not the least little hint, that this is happening. If he did know, he would label it a coping mechanism. He'd be wrong.

"So what's happening with you and Jonathan?"

So that's it. I look sprightly, surprised. "What's happening with me and Jonathan?" I repeat.

"Yes, Elizabeth, that's what I said."

"Oh, nothing much, really not anything, Sid; why?"

"Well, Estelle found him moping in the common room this morning and she drew him out a little, and it seemed that there was some kind of misunderstanding between you two."

I will maim Jonathan for this.

"Misunderstanding? No, not really, I don't think so."

"So there's nothing happening between you two?"

"No, not much."

"Not much?"

"Not much."

"Could you be a little more specific about what you mean by 'not much,' Elizabeth?"

I sigh. I know what Sid wants. "Basically, Sid," I finally say, "Jonathan wants to screw me more than I want to screw him." Sid *loves* this kind of talk. I hope he's not beating off under the table.

Sid can barely restrain his joy at this. "Good, Elizabeth! I'm glad you're opening up! Now, what is your objection to screwing Jonathan?"

"I don't know, I just don't want to right now. I might sometime, I don't know." I find all of this extremely weird and acutely embarrassing.

Tap-tap-tap at the door.

"That'll be Peggy," says Sid. "Come in, Peggy."

Peggy is another MABEE teacher/Sid satellite/member of the adoring fold. She enters wearing a beatific smile and bearing a silver tray on which is a tall, iced glass filled with a frothy chocolate something and garnished with a strawberry cut so it can sit on the edge of the glass. Peggy is wearing a short skirt, high-heeled shoes, a tight blue oxford sweater, and a frilly little apron. She looks like a cross between a cheerleader and a cocktail waitress. When she's not teaching English at

MABEE she's in the nursery, where her three-year-old, Sammy, plays with the other children of women in therapy with Sid, using various psychologically sound toys and games.

Peggy has told me, with great sadness, that her husband, Jeff, is having trouble accepting the "new personal growth" she's been doing since starting sessions with Sid two years ago. "Well, the growth has just been phenomenal, of course, and Jeff doesn't know how to handle it. I've urged him, begged him to start seeing Sid himself but . . ." she paused to shake her head, "but he just won't do it! He's very, very set against this place—can you imagine, after all Sid has done for me? We may, we just may, wind up splitting over it." I feel so sorry for Peggy, who has an open, childlike face and a sweetness about her, who is so totally under Sid's thrall that she would leave her husband over him. She is much too trusting. I feel older than her.

Peggy also prepares all Sid's Weight Watchers meals and special snacks.

She sets the tray down on Sid's desk. "Thank you, Peggy," says Sid, smiling up at her; Peggy's smile increases in wattage. She turns and teeters out on her heels. She reminds me of a little girl playing dress-up, somehow, yet she has a three-year-old son. Only yesterday she invited me, excitedly, into the nursery.

"Listen, Elizabeth, I want you to hear this! Now, Sammy, tell Elizabeth—where . . . do . . . babies . . . come . . . out . . . of?"

Sammy, chubby-cheeked, looked up from a computer toy he was punching, a yellow box with pictures of animals on it and an alphabet, like a typewriter keyboard, in red plastic. A disembodied voice issuing from the toy was asking, "Can . . . you . . . spell . . . dog?" This was immediately followed by some barking sounds.

"Sammy, put down the toy, please," said Peggy, as Sammy randomly hit the keyboard. "No . . . I'm . . . sorry . . . that . . . was . . . not . . . the . . . answer . . . I . . . had . . . in . . . mind. Please . . . try . . . again. The . . . word . . . is . . . DOG!" More barking, Sammy looked up irritatedly at Peggy.

"Sammy, just . . . tell . . . Elizabeth . . . where. Remember? It's what ladies have? Okay, now. Where . . . do . . . babies . . ."

"Pagina!" said Sammy, and went back to bashing the keyboard.

Peggy shuts the door behind her. Sid and I are alone together, again. He lifts his glass and takes a good healthy swallow, then licks his upper lip.

"But Elizabeth," says Sid. "You did give Jonathan encouragement. You did lead him on. Now, either you want a sexual involvement or you don't."

Imagine life being that simple for Sid.

I don't say anything. I know I don't need to; I know very well I'll hear the lecture in any case.

"Elizabeth, people express their fear of sex in many, many different ways. For me, for years, it was eating. I couldn't deal with my sexuality. I was afraid of it. I hid my fears of sex behind a wall of fat."

Sounds like what Camille Peckinpaker told my mother her shrink told her.

"For you, perhaps, your way of hiding is through *thinking* too much, analyzing, intellectualizing, instead of just *feeling*. It's *okay* to have sexual feelings, Elizabeth! They're natural, normal, healthy, *human* feelings! Sex is not a big deal as long as you don't repress it. A few inches of flesh rub against each other for mutual pleasure, that's all."

What did I expect him to say, hefty but no longer

obese Sidney Meyerhoff, guzzling down his Weight Watchers chocolate shake?

"And Elizabeth," he adds, his voice scoldingly coy. I turn from the door as I'm leaving. A thin line of chocolate shake mustaches his upper lip. Click goes the camera.

"Yes?" I say.

"Don't be a cockteaser with Jonathan."

I imagine telling my aunt, "Don't worry, you'll find another couple of inches of flesh to rub with for mutual pleasure real soon."

My aunt makes me tea and an English muffin. It has stopped raining, but the sky is still a deep, overcast gray and it is bitterly cold. Even on a sunny day my aunt's apartment is not bright and cheering, though it *is* expensive, adjacent to Sutton Place, in a well-maintained building with a doorman. My aunt's fairly well off, I think. She owns this apartment. It has a small bedroom and bath, a tiny tiny kitchen, and an L-shaped living room with a dining-room table set into the short side of the L. This is where we are sitting, with our tea in its green and white china pot and its matching cups and saucers and our buttered English muffins, a small buffet table to one side of us on which is an elaborate polished silver tea service. My hands are still cold from walking over from Lexington Avenue; I wrap them around the cup even when I'm not taking a sip.

My aunt's eyes still have that wet, superblue look of the funeral day, but not as intensely. Instead of dazed, she looks fatigued, but determined now, as well. Jay's bed, a single hospital bed with a crank for lowering or raising feet or head, is gone. It occurs to me that perhaps my aunt may have rented it, throughout those long years of siege by Joe's disease. I wonder how long my aunt and uncle slept in separate beds. There's no lingering cigar smell in the apartment, as I would have expected.

I also expect, always, that my aunt would be more meticulous than my mother; but it's the other way around. In my aunt's small apartment, possessions spill over possessions. The bookshelves that line the room are jammed full; books rest on their sides atop the upright books wherever there is room. Every end table is stacked with books or magazines. Paintings, unhung, lean against walls. Curios, little brass or inlaid boxes, carved trees with fruits of semiprecious stones clutter every surface that is not covered with books or magazines.

"Do you miss him?" I ask her.

"Well, of course, knowing it was coming for so long, I was prepared, at least. He was in so much pain, Elizabeth, these last few years, that he wasn't himself. In the early years of his illness, he could still manage his pain, and he was still a lot of fun. But it got so intense. I'm glad he's out of that intense pain."

Is she saying she doesn't miss him? Is she excusing herself for not missing him? Or is she covering up that she does miss him?

Her eyes have a degree more blue to them now. Did I do wrong to ask, "Do you miss him?" I probably have been tactless, stupid.

There's a fireplace in my aunt's living room. It occurs to me that I have never seen it lit.

"Even difficult situations, you get used to," continues my aunt, sighing. "You think you can't bear something and that you adapt to it only because you have to, with great, great difficulty. In fact, while it's happening you don't think you have adapted to it, you think you're fighting it every step of the way; until suddenly everything changes again and you realize that again you have to adapt, whether you want to or not."

She pauses, looking out the windows toward the windows of the buildings across the street. When I have stayed with her, sometimes I see a woman with long brown hair in one of those buildings, directly across the way but down a floor from my aunt's apartment, playing the French horn. Of course none of the notes make it through two sets of closed windows and four lanes of Fifty-seventh Street traffic. "When someone is ill, that long, that seriously," Aunt Pat finishes, "it becomes a way of life for the person taking care of them."

"Katherine was telling me you slept at the hospital a lot."

"Oh, yes," says my aunt. "Not the best way to get a good night's sleep; but I wanted to be near Jay. On the end of the floor, in what they call the solarium, though God knows there hasn't been much sun this year. I used to doze there for a few hours sometimes. Of course it was better to stay in Jay's room, to make sure the private nurses were doing their job." She shakes her head, sighs, then pours more tea, holding the lid on the green and white china teapot as she tips it. It occurs to me that I have also never seen the silver tea set in use. I know my aunt inherited it from my grandmother, who died while I was at Lakeland. I know my mother is jealous because my aunt got the tea set, though my mother doesn't *want* the tea set. My mother thinks my grandmother, her mother and Pat's, loved Aunt Pat much better than her. She's convinced of this. I asked my aunt about this once, and she pursed her lips and said, "Absolutely not. *Patently* untrue. My mother loved Katherine *dearly*. She *never* played favorites.'' I did not ask my aunt again.

Of course, my aunt did get that tea set. And she did say ''my'' mother, not ''our'' mother.

But since I wasn't there, I have no way of knowing.

''Do you remember that time you read Uncle Jay *A Fly Went By?*'' my aunt asks me.

I nod. After all these years, I have finally grown up enough so that it doesn't embarrass me at all; in fact, I feel good that it happened, that Jay remembered it all those years, that Pat remembers it now.

''He liked that,'' she says.

''Are you going to stay here?'' I ask her suddenly, not knowing why.

''Here?'' She looks astonished. ''You mean in this apartment? Why, of course, Elizabeth, where on earth else would I go?''

''I don't know. I just meant, I just thought . . .''

''Well, I may change it around a little, fix it up.'' She gazes around the room. ''Your mother has offered to help me pick out wallpaper and a new rug and some plants—she's so clever at that sort of thing. I appreciate good decorating, but I'm helpless when it comes to doing it.''

I remember my mother showing me, once, the beginning of an essay she wrote in college. She wouldn't let me read the essay, just the comment the professor had written on the top, in a slanted, old-fashioned script, in real ink, now fading: *You have a gift, Katherine. Use it! You can be another Virginia Woolf.* ''I was good,'' Katherine has told me, more than once. ''My professors recognized it, Walter recognized it, then at least, though certainly later, the things he could have done that would have made it possible for me to . . . well. Anyway. Do you know, Elizabeth, sometimes I go back and read those old things, and they astonish me. If they came in at Rahleigh and Byrd, oh, how I'd encourage that young writer! I could have been a genius. I had something special. I did."

I think of my mother writing comments on other authors' manuscripts the way her professor wrote on hers. In the children's-book-editing field I know that she is considered a genius; but that doesn't seem to matter to her; she's offhand about the praise and the awards; she's even offhand, it seems to me, about the ability that gets her the awards.

Katherine writes her editorial comments in green felt-tip pen, her trademark (one of them); green (I'm guessing here, I've never asked her why) because of all the houseplants she has and the garden she loves; green because her eyes are green and because green and blue are her favorite colors to wear. I have seen her so many countless evenings, Saturday mornings, curled up on the couch downstairs, her feet tucked under her, a coffee cup on the table beside her next to a manuscript in its crisp box; reading a chapter of that manuscript, writing comments on the margins of the white pages with their lines of black, carefully typed words, in green felt-tip pen, a thoughtful, indrawn, intense expression on her face, an expression that she wears at no other time.

Of course, if my father is in the living room, he takes the couch, and Katherine sits in one of the armchairs.

I have no doubt she could have been a genius in writing as well as in editing, really in any field she wanted; she's smart, she's determined, she's sensitive, she's strong. What I don't understand is why she didn't do something with these qualities besides help other people develop their talents, if that is not what she wants to do.

"And it's too late now, of course," says my mother, matter-of-factly, when the subject of her early promise comes up. When she brings it up, clearing the dishes from the kitchen table after another one of our interminable dinners alone together in Chilton, punctuating this, like so many of her statements, with sighs.

I know Katherine is lonely. I know she expected one thing from her marriage to my father and got another. I know that, at least sometimes, she hates working at Rahleigh and Byrd. I know she could have been a great writer.

I know she worries terribly that I am going to flip out again.

But I am tired of hearing, from her, about things that didn't turn out.

All of this goes through my mind when my aunt uses the word "clever" to describe my mother. I realize that what I am really thinking about is what I started to think about in Barnes & Noble: potential.

"Did I show you what Katherine gave me?" my aunt asks me.

I shake my head, and my aunt rises, and rummages through her desk, which occupies a conspicuous corner of the living room and is littered with correspondence, calendars, magazines, and stationery. On one corner, in a cylinder of marble, amidst a handful of pens and pencils and a ruler, stands the large brass scissors with which Jay used to pretend he was going to cut off my hair. How odd it is, I think, that objects associated with people remain after those people die.

Of course, to someone else the scissors would simply be a scissors. No association, no cigar smell, no big hand with a ruby signet ring gripping a handful of hair next to the scalp and tugging it gently, no little girl trying to figure out what was serious and what was teasing.

My aunt finds at last, and brings over to me, a large picture frame of bright, tropical blue enamel with gold edges. It's almost the blue of my aunt's eyes.

"I'll have an eight by ten of this done, to put in it," my aunt explains, handing me a picture of Jay. I look at it; then, I stare at it.

Jay's younger face, Jay at thirty-five or forty, still unwrinkled, stares proudly back at me. He has a slightly arrogant tilt to his face, like my aunt gets sometimes. His nose is beaky, with a hook to it. His half smile says *I know something you don't know.*

Well, you do now, Jay, I think, that's for sure. You're dead, we're alive. So what's it like? Did it turn out to have any meaning?

He reminds me of a bird of prey; a hawk, perhaps.

My aunt is pleased when I tell her this. "He was a handsome man," she agrees, though this is not what I have said.

It isn't until I'm going down in the oak-paneled elevator, operated by a Puerto Rican man in an elegant maroon uniform with tasseled gold epaulets, that the appropriateness of my mother's gift to my aunt fully sinks in. I never, *never* would have thought to give a picture frame to someone who had just had someone they love die, but of course it's perfect. The perfect gift. In my mother's choice of that object, I see an understanding of . . . I hunt for the word but it eludes me, as does the insight to choose so well, to fly an arrow to the precise center of the target, which her gifts so often do. That frame, I decide, in these circumstances, has something akin to a religious ritual: It allows Pat to keep Jay's memory alive, while at the same time helping to bury him; the richness of the color honors him and pays respect to him. *It is gone, but it was good, what you had with him;* that's what that frame says: *Rejoice in your memories.*

I know my mother doesn't rejoice in her memories. I know she is suffering now.

Yet despite that, she was able to select that perfect frame. I can recognize my mother's talent for empathy; I lack that talent myself.

Riding in the elevator back down from my aunt's, I am lost in awe at my mother's genius in giving, as I stare at the whorls in the grain of the dark-oak-paneling in the elevator. One of the whorls looks like Italy on a map, an erratic-edged boot.

How did that genius, which I know so well in Katherine, supplant her other genius? "I could have been a *genius,*" she says to me emphatically, as if I were denying it or disagreeing with her, which I most certainly am not. "My professors said I could have been another Virginia Woolf."

Potential again.

But, I wonder, does *potential* genius count?

This question, even to myself, makes me uncomfortable, it seems so intensely disloyal to my mother.

I am a camera, seeing these thoughts, recording my aunt's apartment, the blueness of her eyes, the yellow and gold wallpaper, sprigs of flowers alternated with broad ribbons, in the hall outside her door, the grain in the wood paneling of this elevator, the whorl shaped like Italy.

But what difference will it make if I am unable to, at some point, develop these images I am taking in; print them on paper, cropping out the unnecessary details so that what remains says more than what I actually saw at the time the shutter was open, more than the actual wood grain and eye color and wallpaper, so that everything left in the picture is there for a reason, both asking and answering questions? If Christopher Isherwood had merely lived in Berlin before the war, observing acutely, what difference would it have made? An interesting-enough period of time for him and his friends while it was happening; but his observances didn't make him a writer, his writing did. If he hadn't written it down, no one would have known. Take me, for instance, a seventeen-year-old girl in New York, born long, long after World War II was over; I never would have known about or experienced, secondhand, all these years later, that dark world of cheap boardinghouses and dangerous cafés and the air of impending doom that Isherwood draws so clearly. And I would have been the less for it, less for not knowing Fräulein Schroeder, his sly, touching landlady, or Sally Bowles, his affectedly outrageous sleep-around friend. And the world would have been the less for it, and I think Christopher Isherwood would have been the less for it, if he hadn't written it all down.

The answer, for me and to me, is: no difference. If I want to be a writer, I have to actually write, not just think about writing. Probably, even, I have to publish and put it out there; have companies accept or reject what I write. And, if they accept, have editors write comments on manuscripts in felt-tip or ballpoint or ink pen. And, after that, then reviewers, using phrases like "early promise" if I'm lucky, or not lucky but good, a good writer, and phrases like "rehashing of ancient clichés" if I'm not. And then, finally, it will be the readers' turn, to buy my book or not buy it; and, having bought it, to read it or not read it, to stay up late to finish it knowing that they'll be exhausted in the morning when the alarm goes off but *having* to finish it anyway (just as I *have*, sometimes, to write, or used to). Or to put it down: "You know, I thought this was going to be good from the cover and the reviews, but I just couldn't get through it." And then, after all that, it will come back to me again, because no matter what the publishers and editors and reviewers and readers say, whether they like it or don't like it, I will have to keep on writing, for the same reason I began in the first place which has to do with something entirely inward, yet which propels or compels me outward.

To me and for me, then—and how dangerous this thought is!—potential is not what counts.

Maybe this is why I haven't been doing any actual writing these days, though I used to. If potential is not what counts then what counts must be action, and action has its consequences.

All my life, up to this last year, I wrote. As soon as I knew the alphabet I began writing, at first just pictures with captions, then poems, then short stories, then finally in fifth grade I started my first novel (I didn't finish it; I have never finished a novel, yet I feel novels are what I want to write). At the public school in Chilton, where, in seventh grade, Mr. Beckwirth, who taught my grade English, took me aside one day after class and said, "Now, Elizabeth, tell me the truth; which one of your parents helped you write this, your mother or your father?" At Lakeland, where, in ninth grade, Elaine Devereaux, the youngish black-haired woman who was the drama director as well as editor of *Echoes*, the Lakeland annual book of student writing, invited me to her apartment for orange juice and pound cake, then, laying her hand on the stack of poetry and short prose I had submitted, said, "Elizabeth, I'm going to make an unusual request of you. I want *you* to choose three things, because that's the most I can take from any student, for me to publish. You've given me too much, but it's all so good that I simply can't pick and discard myself. You are an astonishing writer.'' And yet, after saying these words, which by the feelings that rose up in me I knew I had always longed to hear though I had never thought about them before, longed for perhaps as much as my mother did her college professor's comments—yet, after this Elaine added, ''Of course, I understand both your parents are writers as well; I guess talent is just in your genes.''

All my life I have written, much more than I've ever shown anyone, most of which I've thrown out. All my life I *had* to: simple. Possibly the only thing in my life which has ever been simple, this draw to put things in words. The one thing about me worth envying, Tabby had the insight to envy.

What stopped me, this past year?

What stopped my mother?

The elevator man has to remind me, lost in these thoughts, ''First floor, mees.''

The doorman, also in uniform, says to me, ''Have a nice day, miss,'' as he holds open the door. Outside, the cold, ice-pricked wind of another gray November day practically knocks me over. My hair is whipped flat against my cheeks.

A Time to Grieve is still in the Barnes & Noble bag in my purse.

In contrast to my Aunt Pat's apartment, my father's new girlfriend's apartment is huge and perfect and modern and chic. In contrast to my mother's house, which was furnished bit by bit and picture by picture (there's lots of original artwork by children's-book illustrators), which is comfortable and tasteful and interesting but not quite pulled together, my father's new girlfriend's apartment looks like everything was bought at the same time to match. White walls, with large bright graphic art prints in chrome frames; a single tree-sized potted plant, dramatically lit so it throws a shadow on the white wall; a huge squishy white canvas couch perched on a Mexican wool rug in bright red and orange and green; two bright green squishy chairs with red throw pillows.

My mother has lots of little plants she nursed along from cuttings friends gave her. Our couch, which her parents gave her when she and my father were married thirty years ago, she last had slipcovered in light blue about five years ago. She couldn't afford to have all the chairs slipcovered at that time, so they're still in old fabric, a light blue and green plaid. My mother's throw pillows don't match anything else in the room because Dorothy Fiori bargelloed them for her out of kits. One has little red strawberries with green leaves, one has small brown mushrooms, and another has a gray and black cat. Katherine knows they don't match the rest of her living room and is bothered enough by it that if she is going to be working in there for several hours she will gather up the pillows and toss them behind one of the chairs where she can't see them. She always puts them back, though, because she feels Dorothy's feelings would be hurt if the pillows weren't displayed prominently.

My father's new girlfriend's name is Kris, with a *K*. She is divorced and does layout on a magazine my father writes for. She has smooth blond hair, simply cut shoulder length. It swings when she moves. She is wearing a long red hostess gown. She has on a ton of black mascara.

Kris is thirty-four.

My father is fifty-three.

My mother is fifty-one.

Kris greets me like a long-lost friend. "Elizabeth, darling!" She sweeps me up in a hug and brushes cool lips against my cheek, barely touching me. Definitely not a warm fuzzie. I compute quickly that at Kris's age my mother was pregnant with me.

Kris continues, "Walter has told me *so* much about you, I feel like I already *know* you!"

Did he tell her I got expelled from Lakeland for slitting my wrists with a razor? Did he tell her about Tabby, finding me in bed, my tears drying by then as the pills began to take effect, her pulling back the blankets, the sheets, blotted dark red and by then stuck to me, her sober—but not shocked—low-voiced, "Oh, Lizzie, Liz." But perhaps even my father doesn't know that part. There's no reason why he should; just Tab and I were in the room, and in the state that Tabby is in now she may not remember it anymore. Surely my father, who is filling his glass already at Kris's liquor cabinet on which rests an ice bucket with silver tongs, would not, could not have told her much about me? Not anything important, at least. I hope not.

I don't want Kris to know me. I don't want her to know anything about me. I'm prepared to lie.

But if Kris does know my history surely she would not have said, "Walter has told me so much about you."

But if he *didn't* tell her about me and she is not being tactless, she is being phony. Here I go again, my mind doing a hard tap dance with all the possibilities.

"You know, I have a daughter, Regina, who's just your age. I'm sure you two would *adore* each other; but, alas, she's in California with *her* father now!"

How my father could date, let alone rub flesh with for

mutual pleasure, someone who uses the word *alas* in casual conversation is beyond me. How could he go from someone like my mother to Kris? Of course, my mother kicked him out; and they fought all their lives together, at least that part of their lives which I have witnessed, although these fights have been punctuated by occasional spurts of deep delight in each other, delight in the very differences that make it so entirely impossible for them to get along or agree on the most ordinary topics for even a moment. They have been passionately attracted and passionately repelled, genuinely bewildered by the other's behavior. Kris, who came later, has nothing to do with all this, I remind myself frantically, nothing to do with their rough, defective, problematical marriage which I've always known would crash and blow up. And yet they both wanted it. Want it still, but know it is impossible. Against the rugged terrain of their thirty years together, Kris is as flat as a photograph. Meaningless.

"That's a nice rug," I say to her.

"Oh! That!" trills Kris. "Oh, I'm so pleased you like it! I picked it up for a *song* in Acapulco!"

I ask where the bathroom is, but when I get there it's like the day of the funeral: I can't actually throw up even though I want to. I sit on the toilet for a while. A full-length mirror on the back of the door faces me. I examine myself, sitting there on the toilet, starting at my feet, which are encased in black imitation-leather pull-on boots. My black turtleneck sweater is cinched in with a wide gray belt. Over my sweater I'm wearing an open vest knit in stripes of gray and black and maroon. Big square silver earrings poke out of my wiry dark brown hair, which is curly. My nose is big, my eyes are big and blue, with purplish circles underneath them; my lips are full. I have a round, sad face. My skin is pale. I go through phases with makeup. I'm in a non-makeup phase right now but I can see I really need some blusher. I look drained, a vampire's victim. I do not look seventeen.

I get up off the toilet and wash my face with cold water. I open the medicine cabinet, looking for some blush-on. If I find some, even though it'll be Kris's, even though it's tacky to use someone else's makeup especially without asking them first, I'll use it.

Instead, I find Valium and Seconal.

I look at the bottle of Seconal. It's an orange-tinted plastic prescription bottle, with a white childproof cap, with instructions for opening it printed in green on the top.

I am not a child. I could open it easily.

"Elizabeth?" calls Kris anxiously through the door. "Are you all right? Your father asked me to check on you."

Quickly I put the pill bottle back, closing the medicine cabinet as quietly as I can, while I call out, "Just fine, Kris. I'll be out in a sec!"

When I come out my father is standing by the window looking down on Second Avenue. His face, in profile, is tight with worry and misery. A drink is in his hand.

"Actually, I *don't* feel so good," I tell my father.

"We'll leave," he says quickly. "Kris, we're going. I may be back later, but probably not."

"But the other guests haven't even arrived! I was *so* looking forward to your meeting Lawrence and Marcia! And, you know, Lawrence is managing editor at Nouveau now, remember I was telling you about it. . . ."

"Well, but since Elizabeth isn't feeling too well . . ."

"But . . . she just said . . . I thought . . ." Kris is backpedaling, searching for the proper response, the one that will show sensitivity and tact, the one that won't alienate the father she's dating but will bridge the gap to the daughter; I can almost see her mind skimming back through *Cosmopolitan* articles on the subject: "The Care and Feeding of the Divorced Father"; "His Kids: Love 'Em or Leave Him." Finally she comes up with a concerned smile and, laying one burgundy-nailed hand on my sleeve, she says, "What's *wrong*, Elizabeth?"

"Too much Chinese food, I guess," I say.

"I took her to Hing Lee Palace," explains my father.

"Oh *yes!*" says Kris. "Such *divine* food. Alas, I know all too well how easy it is to overindulge there! Your father took me to Hing Lee's only last week."

As we leave the building and step onto the street, my father, taking my arm, says, " 'Let us go then, you and I, . . .' " thus beginning our old, old game of reciting alternate lines of T. S. Eliot's *The Love Song of J. Alfred Prufrock* when we leave somewhere. My father and I have done this for so long that I cannot even remember a time when I didn't know this poem by heart.

" 'When the evening is spread out against the sky . . .' " I continue.

" 'Like a patient etherised upon a table;' " he says. This, I know, is his way of telling me he loves me.

In the cab to Grand Central my father says suddenly, "Oh, my pet, I'm so sorry you're not feeling well."

I'm relieved at this response, for Walter is unpredictable and could just as easily have snapped furiously, "Now why did you have to go and get sick? Stop being so goddamn self-indulgent! Just pull your socks up, Elizabeth, pull your socks up!''

"I'll get better,'' I say to my father. "Don't worry.'' My throat is pulling in, knitting shut from inside. I turn away from my father, who is looking at me with perplexed, helpless concern. I gaze out the window then press my forehead against the cool glass.

"Rough night, ain't it?'' says the taxi driver conversationally. It's raining again, hard and cold.

"Is there anything I can do?'' my father asks me softly.

Face against glass, I shake my head. I whisper, "It's a hard time for all of us.'' My father is in no shape to do anything for anyone, certainly not for me. Over dinner he has told me that he is seriously considering his new shrink's recommendation, shock treatments.

The taxi driver says, "I just hope it don't freeze up on me, that's all.''

When I get to Grand Central I find the correct platform for the train to Chilton. The wrought-iron gate, though, has not been opened yet. I have half an hour to wait. I lean against the wall. My mother is already home. By now she's bathed, in bed but awake, probably reading a manuscript and waiting for me to come home. Since I ate dinner in town with my father, I'm sure she just had cold leftover roast beef and salad with a glass of red wine for dinner. She doesn't heat up food or make a real sit-down meal unless I'm there.

I straighten up and walk away from the gate, wandering through the station. I find myself at the bank of phones across from the bakery where my mother used to pick up éclairs or petit fours for dessert and bring them home with her in their white cardboard box neatly tied with thin white string. She'd hand them to me when she got off the train, at the platform in Chilton, where my father and I would be waiting for her: a treat, a present. That was when we all lived together, before I went off to school at Lakeland, before she and Walter split up, before I flipped out, before I also commuted into New York. She doesn't do that anymore.

In transit.

I find myself looking in the Manhattan white pages.

Your house is on fire, your children will burn.

I can't face her tonight. Can't. Cannot. I stand by a phone booth. I lean against the glass.

Gibbs, Gibson, Gignilliat, Gilbert, Giles, Gillespie, Gillette, Hal H.

I copy down the address and phone number in the little notebook I always carry in my purse in case I should want to write something.

I go into a phone booth. I make two calls. The second one is to my mother. I give her the number where I'll be tonight.

Five

Dangerous Prying

ON THE WAY to MABEE the next morning I duck into a Woolworth's up near Hal's and buy a black and white bandana for a dollar twenty-five. I tie it jauntily around my neck. This is to give the illusion that I'm wearing something different today from what I wore to school yesterday, though I doubt anyone there would notice. My black turtleneck smells a bit under the arms, but I can't do anything about that. I'm wearing my spare pair of clean underpants, the dirty ones now in my purse. At Woolworth's, I also buy some wonderful cheap plastic bangles, eighty-nine cents each. First I pick out a black one, then a gray one, then a cream-colored one, and then I go for it—a bright, bright lipstick-or-fire-engine-or-blood-red one. After all, I think, once it *was* my favorite color. In honor of that little girl; I hope she's still in there somewhere.

I jam the four bangles onto my left arm. Despite the sweater's funkiness, I decide, catching a glimpse of myself in a dark store window, that I look snazzy. I go out into the gray, still cold. The sky has that gray-white look, as though it might snow. I pull my scarf up so it covers my chin as I wait for the bus.

I decide I feel pretty good. Pretty good, yeah, all right!

On the bus going down Lexington toward MABEE I resolve to give my mother a call at work, since I didn't see her last night. I resolve to act nicer to Jonathan. I resolve to call my father and tell him I'm fine, all better, sorry I didn't get a chance to talk to Kris any more and get to know her better. I'd like to say something that's kind or thoughtful or sensitive or polite about the shock treatments, too, but it's not exactly the kind of occasion Hallmark makes cards for. I try on supportive sentences and phrases and finally come up with, "I'm so sorry you're facing that decision, and if there's anything I can do to help, let me know." Sounds good enough, but the fact is I'm as incapable of helping him as he is me.

The good feeling starts to dissipate with this thought, but I quickly pull it back.

The fact is I'm happy because I got away from all of them.

I don't have a "class" till nine-thirty this morning, so I stop at the Deli-World Coffee Shop three blocks from MABEE and get a carton of milk and a bran muffin to go. By the time I get to MABEE I'm chilled through. In the mirror above the ladies' room sink I see I look like Rudolph, the Red-nosed Reindeer, but I decide to interpret my cold, bright pink face as "having a healthy glow." I set my Deli-World bag on one of the tables in the common room, arranging its contents after wiping my drippy nose on one of the paper napkins. I slip over to Sid's side of the complex and manage to get a cup of coffee from the coffee machine, plus an extra Styrofoam cup, plus two packages of sugar without anyone seeing me and interrogating me soulfully, with lots of good healthy eye contact, "And how are *you* doing today, Elizabeth?" This time of morning, all the teachers/patients are with Sid at the morning staff meeting, which is held on the MABEE side. So it is quiet. It is neutral. It is peaceful.

Back in the common room, I bite into my bran muffin. Unfortunately, they've forgotten to heat it up at Deli-World and there's no butter in the bag, so it is sawdusty-dry and cold. But that's okay. Carefully I compose coffee milk by filling the empty cup one-fourth of the way full with coffee, stirring in one package sugar till dissolved and adding milk to fill. Jay-Lynne, the babysitter who once took me to church with her, was the one who introduced me to wonderful, delicious coffee milk, so much better than bitter coffee or bland milk by themselves, pleasantly lukewarm when mixed exactly right, perfect for washing down a dry bran muffin on a good, nondepressed morning after a night with a stranger.

In the quiet common room I start figuring out why I feel good today for a change.

1. I got away from everyone I know.

2. I didn't have to deal with anybody's insoluble problems.

Before I reach 3, I realize that I am doing what Sid Meyerhoff calls "distancing yourself from your feelings by analyzing them intellectually." I also realize that I care less than nothing about Sid's opinion. I know "analysis" is out of fashion as far as therapy goes, but maybe I might like it. My *own* method of analysis, not the Freudian way, not the way that stupid shrink at Hurstview, the first mental hospital I was in, wanted to do it. "If you really work hard," he told me when I was there last summer, "if you really work hard, you might be out of here by the time you're twenty or twenty-five, Elizabeth.'' I was sixteen. How could you possibly get so screwed up in sixteen years that it would take you another ten to straighten out? Although, given my experience later with megavitamin therapy, proving Dr. Prewitt's diagnosis of biochemical disorder, not schizophrenia, correct, no matter how many years they'd kept me there I wouldn't have gotten straightened out.

No, all I mean is, if I'm happy and can analyze why, then maybe I could learn how to reproduce the feeling of happiness.

I get out my morning round of vitamins, grateful, as always, that no matter how unhappy I get now, day to day, it can never ever approach the terribleness of the period before my parents found Dr. Prewitt and got me put onto them. I always keep a couple of packages in my purse, in the little boxes Jay gave me. I continue my mental list of reasons I am not depressed today.

3. I had sex with Hal Gillette. Oh, how pleased and surprised and thrilled he was that I called him and came over! ''God,'' he said, eyeing me appreciatively when he opened the door, ''I sure feel like Christmas arrived early this year.'' It was nice to please someone so easily. He was so delighted with me, and I didn't have to do anything much, at least not anything complicated. Sex: easy.

I swallow the C and the B-6, the E, three or four capsules at a time, saying mentally, ''My throat is *completely* relaxed.'' This little bit of self-hypnosis enables me to get each round of pills over with quickly, today washed down by delicious coffee milk. Boy do I feel good—like my blood is carbonated.

The odd thing is, I feel all this and I didn't even get off with Hal. I hardly ever do with someone, though I did once with Harvey, this guy I met in Washington Square Park after I got kicked out of Lakeland and ran away from home. I stayed with him two or three weeks, until I got caught up with and put into Hurstview. But anyway, orgasms are not a big deal; that I can do for myself, masturbating. Sex with someone else has different rewards. It's so *pleasant* to sleep with someone. Hold and be held by. Stroke and be stroked. Skin against skin feels so warm. It makes me feel that things are not falling apart, temporarily safe. Like sitting near a fire, it warms me. Hal warmed me. And I don't mean just physically. Somehow, when I make love, whether or not I'm very aroused, my feelings always get involved. Though it originates physically, my feelings get touched. Always.

I don't know Hal well or like him enormously but he did give me something I needed, even though he didn't know or understand my situation (because the last thing I wanted to do was to bring in all the complications that had led me to his messy little two-room apartment in the first place). I lied to Hal, almost with every sentence, and that I don't feel good about. But God what a relief! And I gave him something that he needed, too, so it was a fair exchange. And besides, now that we've gone to bed, I can't help but feel a certain affection for him. Good old mashed-potatoes Hal Gillette.

He's not a bad guy, after all. I could do much worse in the casual-screw department than Hal Gillette. Though if I'll ever want to see him again, I don't know. But such a pleasant interlude!

Ralph, another MABEE kid, enters the common room, a record under his arm. Good-bye, peace, quiet, and solitude.

"Hi, Ralph."

"Heh-wo, Whizabit."

Ralph has this thing: He only talks in baby talk. He's fifteen. He also walks with a cane though he has no physical disability. It enables him, at times of stress or excitement, to lift up the cane and say enthusiastically, "Waise cane!" or, sometimes, "Walph waise cane!" He does this a couple of times a day, and it is his sole, solitary joke. I have no interest in understanding why Ralph's variety of being screwed up takes this particularly obnoxious form. Ralph reminds me in some ways of Joshua, this kid from Grace Memorial, the second mental hospital I was in. Joshua always went around wearing a towel over his head. It was draped in such a way that his face and the back of his head were visible, but it covered the sides of his head and his ears.

Before Ralph has even taken his coat off, he slits the wrapper of the album with his thumbnail, slides out the black disc, and puts it on the turntable. As always, soon heavy-metal, hard-hard-hard rock is blasting away. It's always obscure groups I've never heard of, not good classic rock and roll like the Rolling Stones or Led Zeppelin, say, groups that Tabby and I used to listen to on Murray the K. Certainly it's not good poetic vocalist/lyricist jazz-blues-folk musicians like Joni Mitchell, James Taylor, Michael Franks, whom Tabby and I grew into after Murray the K.

Anyway, Ralph's albums have no resemblance to anything I know or like. They're all screechy and jumpy and experimental and arrhythmic, nothing you can dance to or sing along with and think about what the words mean.

Ralph brings in a new album daily. His family is rich. His mother acts in TV commercials. Frequently (actually infrequently, because I don't watch the tube that much) I see her touting Worcestershire sauce. "Wakes up flavor!" she says, vigorously shaking it into a bowl of ground hamburger with a wide-eyed, wildly excited, slightly maniacal grin which strains equally the viewer's credulity and her face. After the burgers in the commercial are made and her TV family is eating them, her TV son says, "Umm-mm, Mom, these are good, what'd you do to them?" Her TV son is not anything like Ralph.

As Ralph's album begins, he sits down on one of the couches across from me and puts his feet up on a coffee table, his cane beside him. "Pwetty, pwetty moosic!" he says. He shrugs his coat off so that he's still sitting on it, lights up a cigarette, and leans back, eyes closed. He has learned the exact maximum volume to which he can turn up the stereo and not bring the MABEE staff running in.

Jonathan enters, holding a white paper bag and a book. I gulp the last of my coffee milk, quickly and furtively scoop sugar packets into the Deli-World bag, crumple said bag around the Styrofoam cups, and attempt to shoot a perfect basket into the trash can in the corner. I miss, but no matter; the incriminating evidence is off the table in front of me and Jon hasn't noticed my disposal of it.

"Well, *hello,* beautiful!" he says as he sweeps in, sits down next to me, puts an arm around me, kisses me good morning. As revved up as I am from my mildly erotic, sensually delightful if nonorgasmic night with Hal Gillette, Jonathan's kisses make me literally shiver, and, well, there go my clean underpants. I squirm, nonchalantly I hope, and I try to look angry; I'm annoyed with Jonathan for getting me hauled into Sid Meyerhoff's office yesterday for psychological interrogation. I want to reprimand him, make him promise to keep any of his sulks relating to me private from now on, but I can't do it. It's being in such a good mood this morning; it's Jon being such a good kisser.

He's not so bad looking, either, I decide, though there is that little gap between his teeth. Today he's wearing blue jeans and a blue sweater and he's looking good, and surely he knows it. He puts his book next to him on the couch; reflectively, I glance at it. *Knowing Heart-Knowledge* by Swami Vereeshuwarala.

"I brought you a present," he says. "Peace offering." Out of the white bag he pulls a package of banana chips. "No sugar, but they're very sweet naturally, and I thought they might help you satisfy that little ol' sweet tooth of yours."

"Thanks," I say. I guess I'm pleased . . . but *banana chips?* Doesn't Jonathan have anything better to do with his time than reform my eating habits?

Still, his arm around my shoulder feels nice. More muscular than Hal's. Can Jonathan smell sex? Does he sense that I am tainted by eight hours' proximity to a refrigerator containing one half-empty jar of mayonnaise and one slice of dried, curling, pink bologna, resting solitary in its sad, slit cellophane wrapper?

(I opened Hal's refrigerator looking for o.j. while Hal was showering. The contents saddened me. I had found solace in the arms of a man with a bereft refrigerator. That edge of loneliness and cold began to blow back in at me at the sight of that bologna; I quickly shut the refrigerator door.)

Jonathan has told me many times that he's extremely psychic. Can he pick up that I've been screwing all night in a drafty apartment on Seventy-first Street?

No way.

Jonathan says, very seriously, "Listen, I've realized that I shouldn't have put pressure on you to go to bed with me; I know you have to come to it in your own time. Listen to this, I was reading this last night, it's far out." Enthusiastically he picks up the book he has brought with him and begins to read out loud to me:

To know Love in Freedom Unfettered
One must know the Bliss of Emptiness, Non-Being.
One must be empty of ego's dancing trap.
One must find the Self through losing the self
Through service to the Perfect
Which wears the face of every soul,
For each soul is searching
To lose itself
To find its Self
To be empty of all but Bliss
To know Love
Love Every Soul
Thus is Perfect Freedom found.

"Isn't that far out?"

Resisting the temptation to say, "Hunh?" I say, "Let me read that to myself, okay?" I read it over, really trying to concentrate on what the author is saying without letting my prejudice against Jonathan interfere. After I read it I ask him, "What's the difference between small *s* self and big *s* Self?

Jonathan, encouraged, says, "Small *s* is the ego; big *s* is the Godhead."

"The Godhead?" I picture a carving of the classic old-man God, complete with long beard, carved on the prow of a ship. Our figurehead, Godhead.

He leans over and kisses my neck, odd punctuation for this lecture. Just on the basis of his behavior today I'm annoyed with him, even leaving out his tantrum yesterday and its consequences for me in Sid's office. I'm annoyed, all right—but still his kisses make my toes curl up.

"Like, a bud is not an immature flower; it's a bud and there's nothing wrong with its being a bud. The bud will have its chance to be a flower."

"Unless it vomits," I say. "That could cause it to drop off the stem prematurely."

"The lips of wisdom are shut, except to the ears of the earnest seeker," says Jonathan airily, implacably cheerful.

Ralph's record ends, and he opens his eyes, gets up, and leaning on his cane walks over to the turntable to flip it over to the other side. In the silence, Jon asks him, "Who're we listening to, good buddy?" I suppose this is his attempt at compassionate spiritual understanding.

"Wough Twade," says Ralph. He holds up an album cover: Rough Trade, in metal studs on the back of a black leather jacket.

I say to Jon, "Just where do you get off thinking you're a flower and I'm some puny little unevolved bud?"

"I didn't say that. In fact, I said quite the opposite. There's nothing wrong with being a bud, Elizabeth, and if you could listen without your ego being involved—"

"Listen, Mr. Lips of Wisdom, you aren't such a picture of non-ego-involvement yourself! Really, Jon, I just can't believe you sometimes, you go around acting like this . . ." *Parody,* I'm about to say. But I stop myself. My compassion? "Well. You can act like whatever you want, but just because I disagree with you you have no right to say I'm not a seeker."

"There you go again, Elizabeth! Did I say that? Why, even Swami Vereeshuwarala says that every soul is seeking, and . . ."

"Look, Jon, I'm the one who requested the goddamn class in comparative religion here, right? Remember that?"

"Yeah, and look who's teaching it! Ann!" He looks at me, chin tilted up a bit, in triumph. He knows he's got me there. The whole school knows about Ann's problems with her mother (she's the one Sid was talking to yesterday before I went in to see him), her active sexual life with three boyfriends, her ex-husband who once, before my time here, went on a rampage through the administrative office at MABEE and smashed two glass paperweights belonging to Sid's secretary, Jean. No, Ann, who only wears designer clothes (if the label doesn't show, she tells you) and carries a briefcase and purse with the little initials of another designer all over them in a pattern I find peculiarly ugly, Ann could hardly be called a spiritual person. Jon has a point.

But suddenly, oddly, I quit being furious, just like that. The whole discussion is so *weird;* being at MABEE is weird, Ralph and Rough Trade, spending the night with Hal—all of it, really, defies my belief in it. I mean, I know this is real life, but how can it be? I remember Tabby telling me that once, when she was little, she had been singing "Row, Row, Row Your Boat" with her second-grade or first-grade class or whatever it was, and she came home from school and she asked her mother, "Mommy, is life but a dream?" "Very seriously," Tabby told me. "I asked her very seriously. I had been thinking about it *deeply.*" And her mother said, "Tabitha, don't be silly, *of course* life's not a dream!"

Mentally, I quickly recap this morning's conversation with Jon for Tabby. Tabby, don't you know I'm rooting for you? Or does that not make any difference anymore?

As I'm thinking all this, Jon has been rubbing the back of my neck with his hand. It feels good. He seems to take my mood change in stride, not even asking me, "What's so funny?" when I laugh; just relieved, I suppose, that I'm not arguing with him anymore. He smiles back, pleasantly; perhaps he feels he's in on some cosmic joke.

"But Jon," I say to him. "Not to bring up a sore point, but aren't you going to have to give up sex if you start doing all this meditation and stuff?"

"Oh, yeah, sure, renunciation." He nods, leans forward, and kisses me very, very lightly on the cheek. It should not be legal, what that light kiss does to me, but Jon doesn't have to know I'm reacting. I didn't feel one-tenth this intensity with Hal last night. Too bad; I think Hal's probably much less crazy than Jonathan. "Oh, yes," Jon whispers softly, directly into my ear, "My days of lovemaking are indeed numbered." Another kiss on the cheek. "This generous offer to most beautiful Elizabeth is good for a limited time only and will *not* be repeated."

I'll believe that when I hear it.

Jean, Sid's secretary, bursts dramatically into the common room.

"Kids, there's an ice and storm warning, and since Sid was planning to go out to Long Island this afternoon and the roads may be getting bad by then, we've decided no school today."

"Waise cane!" says Ralph gleefully, holding up his cane.

Before I leave I call my mother at Rahleigh. Though she is important enough that she's hard to reach by phone, Jill, her secretary, has strict instructions to put me through immediately, always.

"Hi," I say.

"Elizabeth! Hello, darling! Did you have fun with Adele?"

"Umm-hmm." No time to feel guilty about that little lie. The funny thing is she wouldn't mind particularly if she knew that I was at Hal's house, and not Adele's;

that I had sex with him and that he is ten years older than me and teaches at Walden, etc. Though she would mind me lying to her.

I just didn't feel like telling her the truth last night, though at least I did give her the number.

"Listen," I say, "they're closing the school because of the snow warnings, so I'll be going out to Chilton in a little while. Do you want me to pick up anything at the station?"

"No . . . unless you see something at the bakery you want for dessert. And, oh, Elizabeth, I was going to take out some steaks to defrost for dinner tonight but I forgot. Would you mind taking them out when you get home so they'll thaw?"

"Sure."

"And there's fresh asparagus there. . . . Oh, good, honey, we'll have a nice dinner. I'm looking forward to it; it will help me get through this horrendous day. I love you."

"Listen, you might want to leave early too, if it does start snowing."

"I'm planning to go at four if I can swing it and then we'll have the whole lovely quiet weekend together! So I'll see you later, sweetie. I love you."

"I love you too," I say. My stomach churns.

When Hal asked me about my plans for the weekend I said, "I'm all tied up. Family. I'll call you."

Maybe.

I don't remember the steaks until quarter to five. I race downstairs, yank them out of the freezer, frozen together, wrap them in plastic, and run them under the hot-water tap. When they soften up a little I start prying them apart with a kitchen knife.

Then several things happen at once.

The knife slips.

My mother comes home.

The tip of the blade sails into my left wrist.

As she walks into the kitchen.

It's a deep cut; not much blood, but so sharp a blast of pain that I can't catch my breath or speak for a few seconds as I grasp the cut wrist with my other hand.

And she starts screaming.

The knife clatters onto the floor and tears start in my eyes.

Her screams become my name ELIZABETH ELIZABETH.

I'm clutching my left wrist with my right hand and finally my voice comes back and I say IT WAS AN ACCIDENT KATHERINE IT WAS AN ACCIDENT I SWEAR IT WAS AN ACCIDENT.

And she is shaking and sobbing, gone dead white. She drops to the kitchen chair by the table and puts her face in her hand. I'm next to her, saying, "Katherine, Katherine, it was an accident, I forgot to take the steaks out to thaw and I was just prying them apart; it was an accident, it's nothing, it's okay, just the knife slipped, that's all." She nods, but she doesn't stop crying. I reach out and grasp her by the shoulders; they're still shaking, but pain arrows my wrist and I let go again to clutch with the other hand.

I get her a box of Kleenex.

"It's just a scratch," I tell her. "It was an accident, I promise, truly. I'm going to go upstairs and put a Band-Aid on it. I'll be right back down. I'm okay, I promise."

She looks up, her face still wet with tears. "Let me come with you; I can help."

"No, no," I say. "It's nothing, I'll just go do it. I'll be right back down. It's nothing, see?"

And I show her the wound: surprisingly tiny, almost bloodless. I can feel how deep it is—my whole arm is throbbing—but thank God it looks harmless. For its background, on my blue-veined wrist, are the long, pink-white scars, previous artifacts.

"But don't you need some help?" she asks, looking up from my wrist to my face, searching there.

"No, no, absolutely not," I say jovially. "Look, if you'll just get things started here I'll be right back down." I desperately need to get away from her. Just a minute or two's respite from her terrible fear for me and I'll be fine.

"Okay," she finally says, in a soft, preternaturally high voice, almost a squeak.

It's going to be a long weekend.

When I come back down she's setting the table in the kitchen. My mother loves blue, blue and white in the kitchen, blue and green in her bedroom and the living room, blue and red in the dining room and in her study. To set the table she has used the blue reed place mats, the blue and white handwoven linen napkins that one of her authors brought her from Ireland, the shiny blue and white Arabia pattern china she loves, and some hand-thrown pottery bowls, gray with a blue rim, which came from Albuquerque. When the American Association of Librarians met out there three years ago, a New Mexico author of my mother's who writes young-adult novels drove her around the countryside and she admired these bowls in an Indian pottery store. Three weeks later the bowls arrived—the author had sent them as a gift.

Everywhere at our house there are relics from my mother's authors.

Besides setting the table, my mother has put soup on: from a can, but jazzed up with some wine, some herbs, a few sliced mushrooms, and some chopped-up parsley. She has a real knack for jazzing up ordinary food. Once, on a Sunday, some cousins of Dorothy Fiori had dropped by to see Dorothy across the street. But since Dorothy wasn't home they trooped over to our house, dropping in on my mother who was at that time working on a three-hundred-page manuscript by Henrietta Cathcart, a "big" (i.e., best-selling) Rahleigh author who was flying in from California the next day to see my mother in New York.

Katherine smiled, welcomed them in, remembering everyone's name, what they did, where they worked, the names of their pets and kids. She small-talked and then managed to bring out this just incredible tray of odds and ends from the refrigerator that she had turned into party food in about two minutes' time. She had taken one of the blue and white platters, put a mountain of white cottage cheese at one end and sprinkled it with paprika, then laid out several kinds of sliced cheese in overlapping slices. She did a pile of carrot sticks and celery sticks, and little heaps of olives and cherry tomatoes, and a couple of kinds of crackers overlapping, and some ham, and lots of frilly parsley.

It's like giving my aunt the blue frame. How does my mother know? How does she do it?

The day Dorothy Fiori's cousins came my father said to my mother later, "For Christ's sweet sake, Kath, why didn't you just run them off?"

My mother said, "They're Dorothy's *cousins*. Besides, they're very sweet people, and they haven't had an easy time of it lately. Rosetta has to have an operation on her eyes next month; she's scared to death. They took her out driving just to take her mind off it. Naturally they decided to drop in on Dorothy; and when Dorothy wasn't there, naturally they came here. I would have *wanted* them to. They had no way of knowing I was working."

"You could've told them," said my father.

My mother shook her head. "Rosetta needed distracting—she's terrified." To me she said, "You probably don't remember this, but once when you were little Rosetta made you a beautiful, beautiful doll's dress, sort of a coral-salmon color, with handmade lace."

"I remember," I said.

My mother sighed and shook her head. "All her life she's done handwork and now her eyesight is going."

"I'm not saying you should have been rude," said my father. "But Jesus Christ, you could've given them coffee and cookies, talked with them for a few minutes, and sent them on their way, instead of doing a big production. You screwed up a quiet Sunday afternoon, besides which you're going to be up all night now with that manuscript."

And she was. The next day my mother saw her "big" author, Henrietta Cathcart, on about two hours of sleep.

Besides setting the table and turning canned tomato soup into something unrecognizable but delicious, my mother has also washed her face, combed her hair, powdered her nose, and put on fresh lipstick while I was upstairs. When I come back in she smiles at me, reaches out and strokes my hair.

"How's your wrist?"

"Okay. I mean, it hurts but it's okay. It wasn't very deep. We have to talk."

"I'm so sorry I yelled at you, Elizabeth. I know it was an accident; I just didn't realize at first. Does it hurt very badly?"

"Not too. Listen, we have to talk."

"Is it a throbbing pain, or a sharp pain, or more of an ache?"

"Sort of a throbbing ache. Katherine, *we have to talk.*"

It is odd. My mother always, always, always wants to talk to me and about me, but within certain definite though never-stated boundaries. She wants to know everything about me, except what I think of her and our relationship. She wants to tell me everything sad that has ever happened to her in the past, but very little that is either good or in the present tense. And she does not want me to comment or suggest in any fashion that those sad things in her past were things she could have done anything about or changed or done differently. If I bring up something happy, "But what about . . . ," she will sigh and say, "Yes, but . . ." and point out to me all the things I didn't know about that thing I thought was happy that made it, actually, very sad. *They happened* and that's that. And if I were her age and in her position I would understand that. That's that, too.

She may be right. It may be that most of our lives are things happening to us, beyond our control. Yes, I know that's partly true. Certainly the thing that irritates me most about virtually all the shrinks I've met is that they seem to think the complete opposite, that *everything* can be controlled and neatly understood, that there is no fate other than what we make for ourselves. I know for a fact that's not true; but it probably has about the same degree of truth to it that my mother's view has.

Yet Katherine doesn't *live* as if nothing can be controlled, which is why it is so strange. She takes action, constantly. She changes things, she acts on things. When I was in Hurstview, diagnosed as a chronic paranoid-schizophrenic, and she heard about vitamin megadoses, she got me out of there and into Grace and with Dr. Prewitt and onto vitamins. Fast. And, of course, there's her career at Rahleigh: all action, all initiative.

She doesn't talk the way she lives, or the way she lives at least part of her life, which is what makes talking with her so treacherous. And yet I am urging her that we talk.

"We *are* talking," she says logically. Oh, she knows what I want, and she will do anything to avoid it. Why must all direct approaches be seen by her as confrontations? Quick! Up go the castle walls, strengthen the defenses! "Elizabeth, I had a long day, I walked in and . . . I just overreacted, that's all. I apologize for raising my voice; it was uncalled for. I know now it was an accident, believe me."

"I believe you," I say. "But we still need to talk."

"We're talking, Elizabeth, we're talking!" She rises agitatedly and stirs the soup.

"Yes, I know, but I mean . . ." I mean about the terrible fear you live with about me. The burden it places on me, feeling watched all the time, feeling every action weighed and measured for clues as to my state of mental health when I feel your *own* mental health could use some attention from you right now. Your own, not mine, not Walter's, not your authors'. I mean about Walter's absence. Not whether it's right or wrong and every goddamn thing he ever did to you in the past; but now, the present, the two of us, you and me, and what are we going to do, and the two of *you*, what are *you* going to do, you talk on the phone every night about how impossible it is for you to be together. What is happening, why are you doing this to each other? Or is this just another thing that happened, that you and he have no say-so over?

"I mean, Katherine," I say carefully, "about things in general. About what we're not talking about." She is not going to get specific; it will have to come from me. I take a deep breath. "About how scared you are for me. I just feel you worrying about me, and you just have to know that I'm not going to . . ."

She faces me again; she has taken this as an accusation or maybe I have just gotten too close. "Look, Elizabeth! I don't worry! At least, not much. I try—I really, truly *try* to trust you. I do! Did I call you at that number last night? No. Believe me, Elizabeth, I'm making a huge effort. You cannot possibly begin to comprehend the kind of effort I'm making and what it takes out of me. You, your father . . . but Elizabeth, surely you must realize . . ."

The problem is, I do.

The problem is, I know my little mental-hospital vacation cost her forty-eight thousand dollars—the complete, total inheritance her father left her. I know because she told me, just once and seemingly offhandedly; but I know.

Just as I know about the recurring dream she has about me; that was another one she needed to tell me only once.

And I know my parents separated because: because they had to.

And I know my mother is dying of loneliness.

And I can't help her.

But I have to help her.

But I can't.

My mother is so pretty, like Claudette Colbert in *It Happened One Night*, gray-haired unlike Claudette but with that same thin, pert, apple-shaped face and the same kind of figure. To my eye she looks thirty-eight or so, not fifty-one. My mother's eyes are so green, with little flecks of gingery gold in them. But she has been rolled too thin; the dough will come apart, her face will break, and I'm afraid for her but helpless, afraid for my father, for me, for Tabitha, but helpless helpless helpless.

I rise from the table and stand next to the stove.

"Is it soup yet?" I ask her, mocking the TV soup commercial we both detest. She leaps on this joke like a drowning person to a lifeboat.

She opens her eyes wide and smiles maniacally. "I used Worcestershire sauce! Wakes up flavor!"

We laugh.

The problem is, I do love her.

"Is that kid still at school?"

"At MABEE? You mean Ralph? Yeah, he's still there."

"That poor woman." She means Ralph's mother, touter of Worcestershire sauce.

But is Ralph's mother "poor" because she's in the same boat as my mother?

I say, evenly as I can, "What I mean is, you have to really, truly believe that I am not going to make another suicide attempt. That part is over. It's finished."

I said it. My stomach roils.

We're looking at each other hard, my mother and I. Her green eyes sweep my face and eyes, I will her, *believe me, relax, let go, let me go, trust me*, much as I will my own throat not to close when I take the vitamins.

She looks away from me, down at the simmering pinky orange soup in the blue enamel pot on the stove, and she says softly, "I think it's soup now."

It's Friday night. Saturday and Sunday are still ahead of my mother and me, iced in together.

At Grace Memorial, which is where I got transferred after Hurstview, and where I got put on vitamins, there was this kid, Joshua, the one that reminds me of Ralph at MABEE, who always wore a towel over his head. He was younger than me by a couple of years. We never spoke, but of course I saw him all the time, wandering up and down the halls with his towel, a beige face towel, hanging over his head, leaving his face uncovered but covering either side.

Twice a day three nurses handed out pills (or "medication," as they put it) from the windows of the non-breakable glassed-in nurses' station to those who were well enough to line up properly and take it (the others had theirs delivered to their rooms in hypodermics). We would queue up in the hall: Jack, the speed freak, who was sort of my boyfriend at Grace; Mrs. M., whose family owned a world-famous trucking company; Morrie, who was in his late twenties and from a rich family, who had a private room fitted out just like a college dorm room with a stereo, rock-and-roll posters, and plants. He was more or less a permanent resident and was rumored to have had a lobotomy; Charles, who was rumored to be a voyeur; Mindy, who insisted she worked at CBS and was only there for "a little rest and relaxation" (she and I were roommates for a while); and about two dozen others. I was the only Dr. Prewitt patient, i.e., vitamin-therapy case, on the floor. I was one of the first they ever had, and they didn't know quite what to make of me.

Twice a day I was given two tiny paper cups, one filled with the seventeen pills I was supposed to take—the neon-pink C's, the ominous dark brown niacinamides, etc.—and another to fill with drinking water from the drinking fountain. The cups were tiny. I had to stand near the fountain and refill and refill. Even so it was difficult, because with cups that size you really couldn't get a couple of nice big swallows of water to wash the pills down with and other patients resented your cutting back in the drinking-fountain line to refill your cup; and I had a *lot* of pills to take.

I needed a larger cup for drinking water.

We were not permitted glasses, which could be shattered and used to wound ourselves or others, but I had no problem with using a paper cup; it just needed to be bigger. One evening I asked a young, nice-looking intern in tortoise-shell glasses, with a droopy blond mustache, if there was a larger paper cup around I could have.

He gave me a faintly superior smile. "Look," he said. "You know Joshua?"

"Joshua?"

"Joshua, the kid with the towel."

"Oh, yeah, I see him around."

"You know why he wears that towel?"

"No, I don't know why, but all I need right now is a . . ."

"Bigger cup, I know. Now listen. Joshua wears that towel because it's his way of controlling the world."

"Look, all I want is a cup, and I know wearing a towel doesn't control the world."

"No, no, of *course* it doesn't, that's why he's here; but he *thinks* it does. He's made that towel magical. As long as he wears that towel, he thinks nothing bad is going to happen to him."

"So? Look, all I need . . ."

". . . is a cup. You *think*. But what I'm trying to tell you is, you're doing the same thing Joshua is."

I stared at him. Finally I said, "What are you talking about?"

"You think a bigger cup will help you control the world. It will make everything safe. You're imbuing this imaginary cup with magical powers. You look like a smart girl, that's why I'm telling you all this. I figure maybe you can use it."

I paused. I took a deep breath. I said, "Look, I'm on

vitamin therapy, okay, mister? I take seventeen, one-seven, pills twice a day, every day. Have you ever tried to take seventeen pills with a cup about the size of two thimbles? Think you could do it?"

The nurses behind the glass looked up warningly at the sound of my angry voice.

"Hey, pipe down, would you?" said the intern, a little nervously. "Hey, take it or leave it, I was just trying to help."

"Help! If you want to help, just get me an ordinary-sized paper cup, okay? Is that so hard? Don't lecture me about magic! This is physiological, originating in the body, not the mind! I have a hard time swallowing all those pills with so little water, that's all. Simple!"

"Just think about what I've said."

"I'll tell you what I think," I told him. "You know what I think? I think *you're* crazy."

"Well, at least *I'm* not in here," he said, backing away. "As a matter of fact," I said, stepping up to him a bit menacingly, "you *are* in here."

"Yeah," he said, and that little smile came back on his face. "But *I* can leave."

Six

Ice

SATURDAY MORNING Dorothy Fiori drives my mother and me to the A&P, since my mother can't drive. Walking across the porch, down the steps, on the path to the curb toward the car, my mother and I take tiny, carefully balanced steps, clinging to the handrail where there is one. Yesterday's predicted snow turned to icy rain in the night, and there is a solid sheet of dangerous invisible ice over everything.

It occurs to me that even inside the house, my mother and I tread with equal care: The atmosphere is equally treacherous. If one of us slipped, the other might go down too.

Dorothy is waiting in the warm white car, drawn up next to the sidewalk, exhaust pluming into the cold, moist air. There are chains on the tires and the roads have been salted and sanded. Safe: but the sky is overcast and ominous. Anything could happen.

My mother and I have still not *talked* in the way I think we must, or at least, thought so last night. Today the idea of such talk, honest talk, seems as foolish to me as jogging on that invisible ice would be. I feel as though the ice is climbing vertically, slowly encasing us individually. Though we fight it, we're being iced over, isolated, cold, visibility from within poor: alone.

But oh we are so cheerful. At breakfast I ask her what you get when you cross a rooster with an owl; and when she gives up I am happy to say, "A cock that stays up all night," and happy to hear her laugh appreciatively.

"Now that's a nice children's book joke," she says. "Animals . . . just right for the children's book department."

"Speaking of which," I say, "what's happening at the children's book department?"

She sighs. This is what I read as the I-can't-possibly-communicate-to-you-all-the-terrible-things-that-are-happening sigh. "Too much, too much, too much," she says, looking away from me.

"Well, what's one specific thing?" I say doggedly.

"Oh, Elizabeth." Sigh. "It's all interconnected. I can't tell you one thing without explaining something else which requires explaining something else."

"Well, try."

Sigh.

"Oh! Well, here's a story I've been meaning to tell you. I meant to tell you Thursday, but you weren't home. Wednesday, I was going over the new Tania Shavelson picture-book manuscript, which is quite charming and funny and dear, about a little old man, a kind of hermit who sometimes scrounges in the city dump but mostly lives self-sufficiently by himself in a little shack in the woods. He hates people, but he's friendly with everything in the woods. He knows all the trees and plants and wildflowers; he's on a social basis with several deer, a chipmunk, a squirrel, two fieldmice, two owls, a number of robins, a stray cat, a snake, and so on. Well, in one part of the story one of the owls is arguing with one of the fieldmice, and the owl gets angry and swallows the fieldmouse whole. The old man is furious. He grabs the owl, scolds it, holds it upside down by its feet, shakes it, and out pops the fieldmouse, whole and unharmed. And Tania had done such marvelous, funny sketches for this. Well, *Mister* Heindorf . . ."

My mother's lips curl back slightly. Phil Heindorf is her current enemy at Rahleigh. There's usually one every couple of years, then they finally give up and leave for another publisher while my mother remains. My mother says that Phil is a supercilious weasel who is trying to play office politics and worm his way through underhandedness and nastiness into being chosen the new children's book department head, instead of Katherine, the natural choice (besides being a great editor, my mother has also been at Rahleigh for twenty-two years), when the current head, who has Parkinson's disease, steps down. This could happen at any time. Meanwhile, "Phil hisses at me at any opportunity," as Katherine puts it.

She continues, ". . . *Mister* Heindorf had taken a look at the Shavelson manuscript back when I was out so much those last terrible weeks with Jay and Pat at the hospital. Yesterday, I finally got around to reading comments, and written in, so help me, next to the owl story, was, 'Impossible—digestion of fieldmouse would have started with its ingestion by owl—unscientific.' "

"And this is the genius that wants to be head of the children's book department?" I say. I want my mother to feel I am loyal and understanding, capable of following office intrigues week to week, interested in them, interested in her. I want her to talk to me, to trust me, to gradually eradicate the boundaries. I know she doesn't have anyone else she feels she can talk to.

"That's the one, that genius. Well, when I saw that,

Elizabeth, I was furious. Just furious. When I saw that. Well, finally I calmed down, and you know what I wrote in the margin next to his comment?''

''What?''

'' 'Has religious verity: See Jonah, whale reference, biblical.' ''

''Katherine! You didn't!''

She smiles a little smile, quiet, to herself, pleased with this sly, tiny strike. ''Oh yes I did.''

It's the first real smile I've seen her give all week. The first smile I haven't had to tell a joke to get out of her.

''Hi, Kath, good to see you, be careful getting in,'' says Dorothy. ''Morning, Elizabeth.'' I get in back, my mother in front with Dorothy. Dorothy's smell, of cigarettes and faint perfume and Jergen's lotion and hair spray, always seems incompatible with the white station wagon. ''Rough week?'' she asks my mother.

''Terrible,'' says Katherine. ''And you are an angel, just an angel, to come take us out on a morning like this.''

''Nonsense, Kath, the roads aren't that bad; and I had to go out anyway: Martin is coming back this weekend.''

Martin is Dorothy's college-age son.

''Well, Elizabeth and I are so grateful.''

''How are you, Elizabeth?'' Dorothy calls back to me.

''Okay.''

''School going all right?''

''Fine.''

''Good.'' Dorothy turns her attentions back to my mother. I can just sit in the back, not have to talk, listen, cheer, entertain, pretend, convince, hide, or choose to reveal. I let their conversation blur; I don't want to hear anything, just be still, unimpinged on by talk in the five minutes it will take to get to the A&P. Dorothy and I like each other in an uncomplicated way. I am beginning to see how few uncomplicated relationships there are, and I value them a lot. If Hal Gillette gets complicated, for instance, I'll drop him immediately. I have yet to tell him anything true about me except that I want to be a writer: a valuable, important piece of information I would never give to anyone I knew deeply. You have to spread these kinds of things around.

"Liz, did you hear that?"

"What?"

"Dorothy just said she has a sweater at home she wants you to try on."

"Oh, great."

The salt and sand and chains have chopped the ice into slush in the middle of the street. As we clank slowly through Chilton I try to look at the town as if I didn't know it. The big brown Catholic church I was in that once, the gas station with its winged-horse logo (once, beneath that sign, my father told me the story of Pegasus while we sat in the car as the tank was being filled). I look at the mediocre bakery and the expensive grocery store that delivers, which my mother and I try not to use if we can help it, since the A&P is much cheaper. We pass the news and stationery store where once, when I was a little girl and covered head to toe in a shiny little bright yellow rain slicker, the man behind the counter broke my heart by saying, as he handed me my package, "Here you are, sonny." ("But he couldn't *tell* you were a girl under all that raincoat," my mother comforted me later. "For all he could see of you, you could have been . . . an elephant! A tiger! A bear! A dinosaur!" She named animals I could have been that Mr. Rand wouldn't have seen until, at last, I gave up and started giggling, reassured.)

We pass Alphonso's, the mediocre Italian restaurant, and Dickson's Department Store, where Mr. Dickson in the shoe department used to call me "little lady" as he measured my feet on a complicated metal ruler and where Mrs. Bugliano was always pleasant as she brought out sweaters, jeans, and dresses, saying, "We have something very similar in a blue."

If I look at Chilton as if I had never seen it, as if I had never lived here, I guess it's a pretty-enough town.

Mrs. Bugliano had a daughter, Mary Theresa, who was in my class. In the second grade, when I wore glasses (I wear contacts now), Mary Theresa was one of the group that called me "four-eyes." In the third, she graduated to "dirty Jew," to which she would add, with deep loathing, "Didya mother write any more kiddie books lately?" I never tried to explain the difference between writing and editing, but the knowledge of Mary Theresa's ignorance helped me through my fear of her. She could call me names, but *I* knew quietly that I was intellectually superior. Imagine, I would think, holding my head erect at Chilton Elementary, not knowing the difference between a writer and an editor.

While I remember this and many other childhood events so vividly, at the same time they seem as artificially concocted as a movie set, as if I could look behind the Dickson windows and signs to discover only raw lumber holding everything up. But it wasn't that long ago. I'm seventeen now; my years in Chilton were all my life till I was thirteen, when I begged my parents to send me away somewhere, away from Chilton to Lakeland, because of all the school catalogues I liked Lakeland's the best; and they did send me. And at Lakeland I wore contacts and I met Tabitha and I learned that boys weren't some exotic species but easy, easy, easy, and I had sex for the first time and second and third time. And there were other kids, at least a few, who were Jewish, or from artistic or disintegrating families, and sometimes all three; and I was sort of popular with Lakeland's artsy set and three of my poems were used in a stage reading and three in each of two issues of *Echoes*. I think *maybe* I might actually have developed the knack for happiness there finally if the whole biochemical thing hadn't come up: the voices calling *Elizzzz—a—beth! Elizzzz—a—beth!*, the knocking at the door, the way the food tasted, the galloping heart and feelings as edgy and changing as overheard practiced piano scales, jagged, up and down up and down, through a neighbor's open window back in Chilton.

Of course I know *now* it's biochemistry. I didn't then.

It seems like so long since I've fully lived here, went to school here, but it was only four years ago. At thirteen and fourteen and most of fifteen there was Lakeland, then I got suspended, then kicked out, then there was Harvey and the mental hospitals. And now here I am, four months into the age of seventeen, commuting into New York and MABEE on weekdays and returning to Chilton on weekends like today, going shopping with my mother and Dorothy Fiori. And now my parents are separated, and soon will be divorced.

I think Chilton is where the troubles they'd always had began to boil over for them, into what will soon be called, in a divorce court, "irreconcilable differences." My father wanted to live in the city, to stay where they were, in Washington Square. My mother wanted to move to the country, where there was fresh air and she could have a garden, where the family could see the seasons change. My mother wanted a fireplace and a porch. Their little boy, Steph, was nine then, and they had just had a little girl. Chilton was their compromise. The idea was, it was sort of countryish, but close to the city.

But they both lost out on what they wanted. Chilton isn't city or country. I think it's a mean-spirited, unhappy little town where there is prejudice against both Jews and artists; I think its unhappiness seeped in and everything mildewed.

I was the little girl they had. They moved here for my sake.

I have always hated Chilton.

In the A&P my mother says cheerfully, "How about some oranges?"

She hates oranges; I have always known that. When she was a child and had her tonsils out, the first thing she smelled when she came to after the anesthesia was oranges and newspapers. To this day, the scent of either makes her nauseous.

"No, thanks," I say.

"Come on, *you* can eat them, they look like nice ones."

"Look, I can eat oranges in New York if I want. There's even a coffee shop right down the street from MABEE that has freshly squeezed orange juice in the morning. There's no need for you to have to put up with them around the house."

"But wouldn't you enjoy some at home?"

"Not particularly, no." I'd eat them if they were there, but they *shouldn't* be there, since the smell nauseates Katherine and it's her house and I can easily procure oranges elsewhere.

"Oh, come on, just a couple."

"KATHERINE FOR GOD'S SAKE I DON'T WANT ANY ORANGES!"

Hurt, she looks at me, then rolls the cart away. I have ruined the day.

Back home there is a letter from Tabitha. I open it with anticipation and fear.

Hello Elizzie-Liz old sport:

Well I'm still here incarcerated still seeing a shrink still on Valium. I miss you you are so lucky you got out. Did you have a point system where you were? Here it is like living on a monopoly board. So many points & they unlock your door, so many you can watch TV, so many you can go to art therapy and make potholders (not for the preferred type of pot though), so many and you can go to the beauty parler, pool, whatever. Place is huge. Has its own school, fifteen to twenty kids give or take a few being busted and having points knocked back. I have a boyfriend here, Malcolm, he lived for years in England so has a very sexy British accent.

Lizzie I asked my shrink about vitamins, he said he didn't think they would be helpful in my case. I told him about you, he said she's not my patient but maybe its wishful thinking on her part the placeebo affect. I said it couldn't hurt me could it, he said I am your doctor & I say: no vitamins. So that's that. I would have tryed it but you know how they are.

Do you hear from any Lakeland kids? Paul Viguerie still writes me that so-and-so. He's still there.

I love you toots. Don't do anything I *wouldn't* do—do something I *can't* (being locked up here) & write me about it.

Living here proves life *is* a dream, the kind you wish to god you could wake up from.

Love,
Tabbins

Tabby has long blond hair and high cheekbones, and big eyes she used to line with first a line of black eye-liner, then, just above it, a line of white. She chain-smoked when she wasn't in class, and her hands shook. Her laugh had a cough to it because of all she smoked. We roomed together our second year at Lakeland and spent part of the summer between our first and second year together near Provincetown (her parents had rented a cottage), where we pigged out on bacon-cheeseburgers with tomatoes, lettuce, and onions. All month long we ate hot-fudge sundaes, hers with the inevitable coffee ice cream.

Walking down the crowded streets of that salty-aired tourist town, people would call out to her, "Hey, Julie!" She looked that much like the actress Julie Christie.

After lunch I am desperate to get out. I tell my mother I'm going for a walk.

"You'll freeze!" she says.

"It's warmed up some since this morning, and I'll bundle up."

"But it's so slick."

"If it's too slick I'll come back. I just need some fresh air, Katherine."

"Oh." Pause. My mother retrenches. In a small voice which tries to be cheerful but sounds desperately wistful, she asks hopefully, "Well, would you like some company?"

Lightly as I can, I say, "No, thanks."

I go up the street to Emmett's Field and turn right toward Scoville. I have on a T-shirt, sweater, down jacket, tights, corduroy jeans, boots, hat, scarf, socks, leg warmers, and mittens. My eyes, the only unprotected part of me, sting with cold. Since the sky is gray I didn't wear sunglasses, but the white hurts my eyes. It has not warmed up. It is slick.

At the end of the field I take the path that borders the Zinsser estate down to the foot of the hill, where there's a little brook I used to like to sit beside when I was a kid just walking around by myself afternoons after school. But I walk onto the path too confidently; on an icy patch, I lose my balance, slip and fall hard, landing on the base of my hands and my knees. It hurts, especially on the left side where my wrist, injured yesterday, is still weak and sore. But it's more the suddenness of the fall that makes tears come to my eyes. Suddenly I'm crying. I stagger gracelessly, half blind, into the woods, some distance away from the path. I collapse under a tree, a pine, sitting in the snow, my knees drawn up to me with my cold face buried in them. I sob and sob. Other than my own sounds, which I try to keep down, it is deadly still in the quiet woods. Once in a while I hear a car go up Edgers Lane. I stay there, sitting in the snow, crying, till my butt is frozen, maybe ten minutes. Then I get up, take off my mittens, and break through the ice to scoop up a little snow which I rub on my face to erase the residues of crying. The snow feels good, so *definite* in its coldness on my face that it cuts through everything else.

I know you're supposed to feel better after a cry, but I don't.

I'm too cold now to go down and visit the brook, and, besides, my knees feel scraped under my jeans. I head for home.

"D'you have a nice walk?"

"Very nice." Is it possible that she looks even more tense than when I left?

"Your father called."

"Oh." No wonder.

"He would like you to call him back."

Later, after I've talked to my father on the phone, I'm in my room staring out my window at what I have always seen from this window in my bedroom: a square of sky, a triangle of the Nichols' roof, the uppermost branches of a huge maple tree today blowing against the windy gray sky. I can't remember when I have last seen the sun. I know it would be good for me if I started writing poems again, but I can't do it. I've always heard you should write about what you know. But writing about what's happening to me now would be like drilling on a tooth without novocaine.

But I am a camera. I will develop this someday.

Not now.

My mother taps on my door. "Li—iz?" she says. When she makes "Liz" into two syllables like that, for some reason it grates on me like chalk squealing on a blackboard.

"Li—iz?"

"Unh-hunh?" I will myself to be nice, keep the strain out of my voice.

"I have a nice fire going on downstairs." Her voice has that full tone, longing, wistful, that always drives me crazy with sadness and guilt and at the same time makes me want to get as far away as possible from her. "I thought you might like to join me watching it. We could enjoy it together."

"Uh, no thanks." Half of me wants to scream LEAVE ME ALONE. The other half is saying, God, Elizabeth, what a selfish little bitch you are, can't you at least keep her company? You know that's all she's asking and God knows it isn't much considering all she's done for you, considering the forty-eight thousand dollars she kissed good-bye in your hospitalization caper, considering she's probably going to get divorced due to you.

I tell my mother, "I'm, uh, doing something."

As lonely as a child dawdling at someone's locked screen door, she says, "Whatcha doing?"

"Just fooling around with some poetry," I say. This is about the only excuse I can make for wanting to be by myself that will not, I feel, further devastate my mother's feelings. Even though she doesn't yet know I plan to be a writer, she values and respects creative efforts, especially mine—which is in some weird way why I hold back from telling her just how serious I am about writing.

"Oh! Well, in that case I won't bother you." I hear her soft footsteps fade down the stairs.

Tabitha is the only person to whom I have mentioned writing, or the fact that I want to be a writer, who has not then immediately made reference to the fact that one of my parents is a writer and the other an editor.

"Oh, it must run in the family!"

"Well, with your mom being in the business, it ought to be easy for you to break into."

"Carrying on the Stein tradition, eh, Elizabeth?"

"Are you sure you really want to, for you, you're not just trying to win their approval?"

One early fall afternoon, when it was still warm enough to get by with just a heavy sweater and jeans, we walked out into the fields around the school, Tabby and I. It was a sunny day. Her sweater was a nubby hand-knit one, a burnt orange with bits of gold and green and brown in it, much the colors of the flaming trees covering the hills around us. Elaine Devereaux had recently told me that writing must be in my genes, but I must limit the numbers of poems I was submitting, that

I must choose because they were too good for her to choose.

I had stayed up all one night, writing in the boiler room so I could keep the light on without disturbing Tab or letting anyone else in the dorm know I was up, sitting on the concrete floor in my bathrobe, a spiral notebook on my knee, a moth batting around the bulb, working on one of those poems that Elaine Devereaux said originated in my genes.

I said to Tabitha, "See, what I feel is, if I had been born to a sheep farmer and, let's say, a postmistress in some small town in . . . where do they raise sheep?"

"Nevada," said Tabby, chewing on a piece of grass. "Remember there was that missile testing, or nerve gas, or something in Nevada and all those thousands of sheep died, and the next spring most of the lambs were born mutated?"

We both shivered.

"Well, Nevada, then," I said. "Let's say I'm born there, a sheep-farmer's daughter; I still feel I would have been a writer. But how can I prove that to someone?"

"And why should you have to?" Tabby asked me. "Why should you?"

We had arrived, by this time, at a flat, gray, rock ledge about two-thirds of the way up one of the hills surrounding the school's acreage. We sat. The sun had warmed the rocks, and it was still at an angle where it shone directly on us. The light glinted almost blindingly off Tabby's yellow hair, and she threw out the stalk of grass she was chewing on, picked another one, and began to chew on that. She leaned back on one elbow, squinting up at the sun, then shading her eyes with one hand. We sat, companionably quiet for a while. I took out a Tiger's Milk candy bar that Katherine had sent me, unwrapped it, split it in two, gave her half. The mock-chocolate coating was melty in the sun, the peanut buttery filling sweet and chewy. Wordlessly, we ate it.

"People are just too eager for the quick fix, you know, Liz?" She frowned, not looking at me, continuing to squint up. "Easy explanation. Easier to say 'Elizabeth Stein wants to write because her father does,' than to say 'Extraordinary work for a sixteen-year-old, rare talent, unusual, beautiful, crazy poems, a miracle a young girl could have written them.' "

I didn't say anything.

"People," she said, "will choose the mediocre and the mundane over the miraculous any day."

Later, walking back down the slope, she said, "You know, I bet the army scientists who set off that nerve gas or detonated that bomb had such wonderful reasons why what they were working on was more important than killing and maiming a lousy bunch of sheep."

When I called my father back after I went out walking, he told me that he'd decided to take the shock treatments, definitely, for sure.

It is this that I am thinking about as I lie on my bed in Chilton, staring out the window at the swooning leafless maple tree.

His doctor recommended a series of eighteen shock treatments.

His doctor said he should have someone waiting afterward to take him back to his apartment following the shock treatments. Since his friend Saul Wermer was out of town and Paul Hoenig was in the hospital having a prostate and Kenneth Gehman was out on the Coast doing a treatment based on his last novel, and since he didn't want to ask his girlfriend Kris and since he could hardly ask Katherine under the current circumstances, would I come and wait for him at the doctor's office on Tuesday, catch a cab with him, and take him home?

Sure.

"And don't tell your mother you'll be doing this, okay?"

Sure.

As I watch the maple tree blow, I remember what Jack, my sort-of boyfriend, the speed freak at Grace, told me about shock, which he had had.

"You don't remember it afterward, you don't know what happens, but you have this fear. It's like, it was so bad, so terrible, that you never want to have it again, but you don't know exactly why and that makes it worse."

"But does it make you feel any better afterward?" I asked him.

Jack, blond and painfully skinny, eighteen, paused, considering. "No," he said. "Different, maybe, but not better."

Before dinner, my mother says, "I'm sorry I reacted that way at the A&P this morning."

I say, "I'm sorry I yelled at you about the oranges."

"I love you."

"I love *you.*"

But I still wonder what happened at the A&P. Do I drive her as crazy by trying not to accept as she does me by giving relentlessly?

At dinner:

"Do you know your father's thinking of having shock treatments?"

I nod. Funny, the way it's always "your father" these days.

"What do you think?"

I shrug. Then I ask her, "What do *you* think?"

She sighs. And I can't even attempt to diagram this sigh; it encompasses too much, the enormity of disintegration moving inward on her from all sides. "I hope it helps him," she says.

Seven

The Hope, Promise, and Safety of Today's New Electroshock Therapy

On Tuesday morning I call my father from the Deli-World Coffee Shop. I don't want anyone at MABEE listening to my conversation with him. He gives me the address of the doctor who will be performing the shock treatment, which I write down in a small spiral notebook.

"You may recognize the office when you see it," he says to me casually. "It's that nice Dr. Phipps, the one who got you back into Lakeland."

"Dr. Phipps?" I say, unable to hide the dismay in my voice. "Dr. Phipps is giving you shock treatments?" The noise of the coffee shop, clanking silverware against thick china, bustles around me, ordinary and busy.

"Unh-hunh," says my father cheerfully. Unlike my mother, who is sensitive to every new emotional nuance, a blink, a tightening of the mouth, stress laid upon a particular word, my father misses my fear completely. "Yes," he continues, "Dr. Phipps. I'm very optimistic. I've always been grateful to him for seeing you that time. He has a new book out, *The Long Return*, subtitled *The Hope, Promise, and Safety of Today's New Electroshock Therapy in Curing Chronic Depression.* I read it; it's pretty good. I went to see him and asked him if he thought I could benefit from the treatment and he seemed very sure I could."

"But," I say, "I thought it was your regular shrink, the new one, who recommended the shock; you know, the guy you've been seeing since you left the behaviorist?"

"Oh!" laughs my father. "Oh, Schmidt, the gestalt guy! Oh, no, I quit with him several months ago. Can you believe this, Elizabeth, he thought I had a *drinking* problem! He wanted me to do things like pretend to talk to a bottle of Johnny Walker Red, for chrissake! I have never in my *life* felt more ridiculous than I did in that doctor's office, having this imaginary conversation with a bottle of Johnny Walker Red!"

I don't say anything.

"So anyway, Elizabeth, I'm very optimistic about this. I have the utmost faith in Dr. Phipps. I'm sure this'll help whisk away those ol' blues yo' daddykins has been feeling—though, I don't know, maybe it's part of the writer's temperament, depression, like booze and coffee and cigarettes, like wine, women, and song. Well, we'll see. We'll give it the old try. We'll run it up the flagpole and see if the general salutes it."

Signal for another one of our lifelong routines. Slowly I respond, "We'll put it out on the back steps and see if the cat licks it."

"We'll toss it in the air and see if it flies."

"We'll throw it against the wall and see if it sticks."

I cannot believe we're talking in these terms about shock treatments for my father. I feel sick again, but I already know I won't be able to throw up.

"So you'll be there at four?" he asks me.

"Yes."

Only then does the faintest note of anxiety creep into my father's voice. "Lizzie?"

"Unh-hunh?"

"Dr. Phipps says there's a chance I might be a little, oh, kind of spaced out afterward, you dig?"

Because my father was a semibeatnik in the forties and fifties and a jazzwriter (he played jazz piano himself before I was born and he has written articles about people like Ella Fitzgerald, Benny Goodman, and Duke Ellington) he occasionally comes out with phrases like "you dig." Because even now he reads *Rolling Stone*, he also uses phrases like "spaced out." A lot of times *Rolling Stone* phrases pop up in his speech, too: groovy, freak-out, bummer. He has no idea which are in current use. It doesn't matter to him. If he uses a word, then as far as he's concerned, it's current. My father is the type of person the party doesn't start without. Makes his own rules, fashions, trends. Tells jokes, well. Recites poetry.

That's one side of him.

He says, "So if that happens, don't freak out, okay?"

"Okay," I say.

"Groovy," he says.

All I can think is: Dr. Phipps.

One of the things I've read over and over in psych books is that a suicide attempt is a cry for help.

In my case, I did a lot of crying for help before I got around to Seconal, Valium, and the razor.

I didn't tell anybody about the voices because that was too, too weird, but I did go to my guidance counselor at Lakeland, a Swiss woman named Trudy Jurgen, about the moods. By that time, my sophomore year at Lakeland, my hands were starting to shake almost as badly as Tabby's, and food was starting to taste funny so that

I was eating less of it. But it was the mood swings that terrified me.

I went to Trudy of my own volition one February afternoon, went to that tiny office that looked out onto the barren New England landscape, gray sky, white fields, leafless skeleton trees, and I said, plainly, simply, unsymbolically, overtly, "I need help."

Trudy tapped her pen on her desk. She didn't say anything. A small woman with graying brown hair which she wore pulled back, she also taught at Lakeland. She was a very, very good teacher. I still remember distinctly a class where she outlined Buddhism, writing its precepts on the board in a clean, sure print, the chalk never squeaking. "The first Noble Truth," she said, "is that life is suffering." She wrote "life is suffering," on the board, then turned to us, hands on hips, and said, " 'Duhka,' that was the Buddha's word for suffering. Life is suffering. Now why, why would the Buddha think life is suffering?" I still remember the class discussion of that and the other three Noble Truths of Buddhism. That was what I wanted when I asked for a comparative religion class at MABEE; but Ann, who teaches it here, wouldn't know a Noble Truth if it goosed her in broad daylight.

I say all this to explain that I liked Trudy, trusted her, respected her. Otherwise I could not have gone as far as I did. After I said I needed help, she remained quiet, just tapping her pen and looking at me. I tried again.

"I'm in trouble."

At that she leaned forward, eyes drawn together, scowling (which creased her face deeply), and replied, in her clipped, stern accent, "You're not pregnant, Elizabeth!"

"Oh, no. Different trouble."

Tap-tap-tap-tap and that intense stare, almost a glare.

"Am I interrupting you, Trudy?" I finally asked.

"Just go *on,* Elizabeth, I'm *waiting.*"

Even her impatience didn't stop me. "It's feelings. Everything is going right for me this year but I just . . . sometimes . . . my hands shake and I feel like . . . I can't control it, whatever it is, and I don't understand it, see? Everything outside me could be fine but inside I just feel like . . ."

I trailed off; again she did not speak. I began a third time, now speaking rapidly.

"Okay, this is crazy, but one minute I am happy, I feel good, I'm splashing the cologne my mother gave me on my wrists and everything seems great; and it could be just maybe like an hour later and I'm looking down at those same wrists and everything seems so bad, just so bad, even though nothing has happened to me in that hour to make me feel that way, that I just want to . . . I mean I see my wrists, they look so white, I can see the blue veins, it would be so easy, so easy to cut them open."

"Don't you think that's a bit melodramatic, Elizabeth?" Trudy's dry voice made me squirm with embarrassment.

"Yes I know it is, Trudy, I know, but that's how I feel, and I don't know what to do and I'm really getting scared!"

Trudy stood up. "Come," she said dryly. "It's not as bad as that. You must remember you are a teenager, which brings with it much . . . overdramatization." With a wry smile she said, "What is there to worry about, Elizabeth? After all, either you'll slit your wrists or you won't."

I had brought fifteen or twenty Seconal back to school after winter break. A good medium for trade at Lakeland, I had nipped the Seconal from the medicine cabinet at home. Both my parents had prescriptions; neither noticed they were ten or twelve short. I had traded out several, for favors, for joints, but I still had five left. A week after my talk with Trudy, I took them all.

After I talk with my father I walk back to MABEE, where Abby says to me, "You seem depressed today, Elizabeth."

Of all the things that I do not want today, to be sent into a tête-à-tête with Sid ranks first. A cool, mentally healthy cover is essential.

"No, just thoughtful," I say, with what I hope is a convincingly thoughtful smile.

"You sure?" Abby asks.

"Unh-hunh," I say pleasantly. "Why?"

"Sometimes 'thoughtfulness' can really mean 'depression.' " I can practically hear Abby's quote marks. Abby's one of Sid's stars.

"Sometimes," I say, "thoughtfulness can also mean 'full of thought.' "

"True," says Abby with a smile. "Just remember, Elizabeth, everyone here truly wants to help you. But no one can help you if you don't want to be helped."

"I'll remember that, Abby," I say.

After I took the Seconals and slept them off (that time I didn't have to have my stomach pumped) my father came up to get me at Lakeland. I was suspended. I would not be allowed to return to Lakeland unless I had a "psychiatric evaluation" which proved, as my father put it, "that you're not going to do another number like this." Outside of this, I don't remember the two of us speaking the whole three and a half hours down to Chilton. It was February, the sky was gray and the roads icy. We passed few other cars on the turnpike. My father drove with extremely tense concentration.

Dr. Phipps was the doctor they had found to conduct my psychiatric evaluation for Lakeland.

Because I roomed with Tabitha, because I loved her, she was the one I came closest to telling, besides Trudy Jurgen. Tab saw me, one night, get up and open the door, look down the hall, come back in, and close the door. After the fourth time I did this, she looked up from her fingernails, which she was painting carefully in stripes of purple and bright green, and she said, "What are you doing, Lizzie?"

I hesitated, then said lightly, "Oh, I keep thinking I hear footsteps down the hall, then these faint knocks on the door; but when I get up and look there's no one there." I paused, then shrugged. "I guess I must just be paranoid."

Tabby, sitting on her bed, looked across the small room to me sitting on mine. The dorm rooms were made of painted-over cinderblock, but each bed had a huge cork bulletin board on the wall beside it where you could put up stuff. Mine had posters and proofs of children's-book illustrations my mother had sent me. Tab's were covered with photographs, posters, pictures, and cards of her three favorite animals, pigs ("because I eat like one"), butterflies ("because I keep hoping I won't be a worm forever"), and unicorns ("I know!" I told her, "Because you're always horny!" "Always horny, but always *singly* horny!" she said).

So Tabitha sat beneath her pigs, butterflies, and unicorns, and looked at me. Then she looked down at her nails and said, very softly, "Don't feel bad, Lizzie, I see things in trees."

She began to blow on her nails, drying them. Despite how badly her hands shook, she could always do her nails perfectly: never a smear or smudge, never a drop on the cuticles.

I never asked her what she meant about the things in trees.

I will tell you the truth as I now understand it: I wanted to be normal; I knew I wasn't. I couldn't speak or give name to what was wrong; I wanted someone to figure it out, to figure out at least that something *was* wrong since I couldn't say it. Because at the same time that I wanted my illness named and treated, I was also desperate to not let anyone know how really crazy I was.

At seventeen, now, people guess me to be in my mid-to-late twenties. Self-possessed. Hal Gillette, for instance, thinks I'm twenty-seven and live in an apartment in the Village which I will not give out the address of. He thinks I write and do part-time secretarial work for a living.

When I was fourteen and *crazy*-crazy, I was equally convincing, equally mature in my artifice.

Back in Chilton, after Lakeland suspended me, the atmosphere was leaden with my parents' unhappiness and their disappointment in and worry over me. Katherine was having troubles at Rahleigh, and a well-known comedian who had hired my father to ghostwrite his autobiography decided, after my father had written it, that he didn't want it to be published. I hated Chilton. It was gray every day. That period all blurs together into two or three weeks of unhappiness, one of those periods, like later on at Hurstview, of which I have few specific memories, only an overall feeling, bleak, watercolors in blurred shades of gray. My father, who worked at home, was so depressed by the comedian's rejection of his book that he was able to do little writing, and was making almost no money. Thus, it was absolutely essential that my mother go in to Rahleigh. For this I was, selfishly, glad. As it was, she called me at home from Rahleigh five or six times a day: How was I doing, what was I doing, was I having a good morning, what had I had for breakfast, what was I wearing, oh yes, that blue sweater brought out the color of my eyes beautifully. I knew she loved me: That very love and concern cut me as sharply as the razor I was to use in my next suicide attempt, the one where Tabitha found me, the one that finally got me expelled permanently from Lakeland.

But then, after the first try, I was desperate to get back to Lakeland, away from Chilton.

I cannot remember what Dr. Phipps asked me during my evaluation, only that I managed to end each reply with " . . . but if I get back to Lakeland that won't be a problem," or " . . . and that's why I want to be at Lakeland."

I was telling the truth; I was lying. I was an onion, layers and layers and layers under a thin, papery skin. If anyone had been able to cut me open, my bitter, irritating juices would have stung their eyes, and they would have cried. Although I couldn't cry, myself, much at the time.

But no one could cut me open.

After twenty minutes, Dr. Phipps buzzed his secretary. "Iris," he said, "get me . . ." Hand over the phone he said to me, "What's her name again? The guidance counselor?"

"Trudy, Trudy Jurgen, at Lakeland School, your secretary has the number."

"Trudy Jurgen, at Lakeland School," he said into the phone. He held the hook down and smiled at me, wordlessly. The phone buzzed.

"Hello, Trudy Jurgen? Dr. Leo Phipps here in New York. I have Elizabeth Stein in my office now. Yes.

Yes. Unh-hunh. Well, I have good news for you. *Elizabeth is nothing but a silly-billy.*"

My heart sank. I had managed to fool even a professional.

Did Tabby also hear the voices calling her name over and over? Taa—bee! Taa—bee! Taa—bee! Or maybe, Taa—bith—aaa! Taa—bith—aaa!

Does she still hear them?

There are some questions you cannot, cannot ask, even your best friend.

At four o'clock Tuesday I'm in Dr. Phipps's waiting room. Dr. Phipps bustles out first. "Well, well, *well,* Elizabeth, nice to see you! Your father's just *fine,* he'll be out in a second! And how are *you? My,* you're looking well! I understand that you're now at school here in the city! Everything going well? Good!"

The waiting room is full. Dr. Phipps speaks to me loudly. A few of the people waiting idly look up, but most just stare ahead.

My father comes out, walking slowly. He looks pale and dazed, unfocused. Something inside of me is crumpling, tearing, twisting as I watch him. "Well, Walter, how are you!" says Phipps jovially, as if he hadn't just spent the last half hour running voltage through my father's brain but was seeing him for the first time in ages, an old friend by the hors d'oeuvres table at a party. "Say hello to your daughter *Elizabeth* here, tell *Elizabeth* you're feeling fine. Now, Walter, you'll start noticing some improvement after the next three or four treatments, and from then on you'll just get better and better!"

"Lindbergh!" calls the nurse at the reception desk, and an older woman stands and pulls a dark-haired, dazed-looking girl of maybe eighteen to her feet, propelling her toward Dr. Phipps.

"Well, Linda, how are you today? Ready for your next treatment? *My*, you're looking well—you get prettier and prettier! Well, come on in!"

Before the door closes behind Linda and Dr. Phipps I catch a glimpse of the room, the same one my father emerged from. A white examining table, straps, some strange headgear, three or four nurses in white standing around the table. The sight chills me to the marrow of my bones.

"Hi, Elizabeth," says my father very slowly. "You . . . ready . . . to go?"

"Oh, Daddy," I say. I hardly ever call him that. I hug him, feel his scratchy tweed jacket under my cheek. He vaguely pats me, then his arm drops.

"Are you all right?" I ask him.

"I'm . . . all right."

"Here's his coat," says the nurse. I get him into it and we step out into the cold. I say, to cheer him, " 'Let us go then, you and I, when the evening is spread out against the sky . . .' "

He makes no response.

I walk us to the corner of Park and Sixtieth where I catch us a cab easily, and I take my father home to the Belle Epoch Apartments, where he has lived since he moved away from Chilton, my mother, and me.

From the Belle Epoch, on extremely east Forty-seventh Street, it is five short blocks down to Forty-second, and from there several long blocks across to Grand Central Station. I have my hat pulled way way down over my ears and my scarf wrapped around my mouth and my dripping nose. The wind cuts right through my pea coat "just like a giant razor blade blowin' down the street,'' as one of my father's jazz albums, by Lou Rawls, puts it. I walk briskly, counting the long cross-town blocks; from First to Second is one, from Second to Third, two; from Third to Lex, three; from Lex to Park, four . . . and there is Grand Central. The whole landscape is in gray and black, except for the brightly lit, colorful shop windows.

I call Jonathan, who is at home in Riverdale.

I call my mother and leave her Jonathan's number, where I'll be tonight.

Eight

At Riverdale

JONATHAN'S PARENTS are off in Europe somewhere, and in that whole house, much bigger than ours in Chilton, there's only Jon and me. The maid has a garage apartment, but when Jon's family is gone she stays with her family in Yonkers and only comes in two days a week. I don't get to Riverdale till after eight o'clock, and when Jonathan opens the door I kind of fall into his arms like a tree right after the lumberjack has yelled "TIM-MMBERRR!"

Jon starts kissing me right in the doorway, and pretty soon we're making love on the carpeted floor of his parents' rec room. It feels so good to be that close to another warm, living, moving body, *close without words or explanation*—that's the key. I keep hugging Jonathan, I'm freezing cold and he's the fire and I want to get closer and closer. I keep praying he won't say something stupid and ruin it. He doesn't. Of course, I don't come with him, but I never do with anyone, except that one fluke time with Harvey, so I don't mind.

To my utter shock, therefore, Jonathan says to me

softly, with great concern, after we've made love, "That wasn't very good for you, was it?"

I'm astonished. "Good? It was fine, Jon, fine, I enjoyed it. No complaints."

"Well," he says, "we'll see if we can't do better this next time." And then he amazes me by beginning to make love to me *again,* then and there, with great tenderness and attention and an astounding amount of technique. Jonathan, who I had prayed would not talk, whispers to me in the dark as he's caressing me so slowly, a nonstop stream of reassurance and praise and light porn punctuated by those sweet, delicate, breathless kisses which turn me on infinitely, so much more than heavy, hard-core, grinding mouth-to-mouth kisses. He kisses my mouth, my neck, my ears, my shoulders, my breasts, each fingertip of both hands, as he's murmuring and stroking. "Oh, Elizabeth," kiss, "you're so beautiful, so lovely," kiss, "I really love your breasts, they're so responsive," kiss, "so smooth and beautiful," kiss, kiss, kiss, "you know I've looked forward to making love to you since the first day I saw you," kiss, kiss, "you're so tight, but I'm gonna make you so loose," kiss, "I'm going to make you so loose and relaxed and responsive and turned-on, Elizabeth, I'm gonna make you let go," kiss, kiss, kiss, "your jelly is gonna flow, and your nipples," kiss, kiss, "they're going to get big and hard just like they're doing now."

"Oh God, Jonathan, what are you doing to me?" I murmur. I have never, never felt like this before. Absolutely melting. Even my blood has heated up.

"Just what you've been doing to me for a month and a half, baby, I'm turning you on, like you've been turning me on. But you don't mind, do you?"

He keeps this up for maybe twenty minutes, talking,

caressing gently and with deadly anatomical accuracy. When he finally enters me a second time and begins moving with very slow, long, deliberate strokes, I come like I have never come in my life.

So why do I wake up in panic in the middle of the night, sitting bolt upright suddenly in the bed in Jon's room, my heart beating rapidly, feeling like I can't breathe? Jonathan lies sleeping beside me obliviously, on his side, back turned to me. His dark hair is splayed upon the pillow, and sheets and blankets cover him except for one vulnerable exposed pink-apricot shoulder—and even the sight of that shoulder makes me shiver with turn-on again. Yet this is dwarfed by the mountainous overwhelming sense of panic that has woken me from a sound sleep.

I sit there in bed next to Jon for a few minutes. I know logically that I must be breathing, but it doesn't seem like I am. It feels as though I can't get my lungs all the way full, and my heart is thrashing against my ribs like a bird caught and tangled in a net. I feel panicked, terrified: a nightmare-deep terror, yet not attached to any particular thing or reason. Am I reverting? Should I get up and take an extra round of vitamins? I listen, filled with dread, to see if I can hear my name being called, however faintly. But all I can hear is the wind in the trees, a branch tapping the house lightly. The voices are silent, as they have been since a month after I started vitamin therapy. So, then, this is not biochemistry, but me, myself, my head, my feelings. I have somehow trapped myself on this island, pounded by hurricane waves of reasonless terror.

Of course I can think of perfectly good reasons for panic.

1. My father.

2. ·My mother.

3. Tabby.

But in a weird way these seem beside the point. This anxiety feeds on itself, a large, fast-growing cancer.

Chilled, very wakeful, I slip out of bed. Jonathan's room is illuminated by the ghost-white light of a street lamp. Jonathan himself does not stir, except for his heavy, regular breathing. I find a terry-cloth robe in Jonathan's closet and put it on. I'm scared to wander through this strange, dark, empty house in Riverdale, New York. My heart steps up its pace even more when I merely go down the hall to the bathroom. I find my legs are weak, faintly and pleasantly sore from that mind-boggling lovemaking before; and with that thought, I get another wave of turned-on-ness, followed by a sharp jab of anxiety. I come back into Jon's room, which is white, austere, decorated only by a print of one of those circular Tibetan drawings with clouds underneath and hundreds of tiny drawn-in figures of animals, gods, and goddesses. The plush carpeting, a light green, is in every room of the house, but over it, in his room, Jonathan has placed a thick, scratchy jute mat.

That underlying carpet is the same carpet Jon and I made love on, downstairs. Oh-oh. And that shoulder of his. Oh Jesus, oh Jon, I'm opening again. This is going to be a problem. Anything strong is a problem. This is as strong as an undertow that could take me out to sea forever.

One wall of Jon's bedroom is filled with a built-in bookshelf. At eye level on it are several packages of incense and a couple of books of matches from a restaurant called Taste of India. Books, too: *Gems from the Tibetan Masters. The Eternal Now. Wisdom of the New Age. Swami Pravalarendarala's Guide to Holistic Health and Meditation. Yoga for the Whole Life. The Dance in the Garden: Sufi Sayings. Acupressure for Relaxation.* And then, surprisingly: *How to Win Friends and Influence People, Roget's Thesaurus,* and *How to Pick Up Girls.* Oh, Jonathan! I suppress a laugh, smile instead in the semidark.

(If I ignore the panic maybe it will go away.)

At floor level on the bookcase, in the far corner, are: *Winnie the Pooh, Stuart Little,* and *Charlotte's Web.*

I have a roil of anxiety, a choking wave of it, as I think of the Jonathan that read those books, who has vanished as surely as the solitary child who played alone for hours with my dolls: Sandy, the tomboy; Marietta, her sidekick; Meg, the poet; Gwendolyn, who was conceited, and the others, who all lived in their orphanage overseen by the kindly Miss Flora on bookshelves in my room in Chilton.

I made tiny books for my dolls of stapled paper, copying stories for them in printing which was as small as I could manage.

I could never understand how two people together could "play dolls." How could you ever explain to someone else everything you knew about your dolls, their lives, their tastes, their backgrounds, and what made them feel as they did? Sometimes, now, for these same reasons, I doubt two people can do anything together; the amount of explaining necessary makes it impossible.

The children Jonathan and I were are now vanished: My Uncle Jay, who gave me jewel boxes for my dolls, is gone even more entirely. He's only a picture in a blue frame, a handful or two of ashes, and, perhaps, what various people remember of him.

Jon and I, sixteen and seventeen, made love earlier tonight with practiced and savage skill in the same room where Jon, as a child, once read. My parents made love, and Jon's did, for pleasure, of course, and also to make us. But how improbable it seems that they could have ever felt this impatient, crawling, invasive urge that is taking me now like the flu, erotic viruses procreating madly in my blood. Oh, Jon, now everything is complicated and I did not want more complications. And you're still sleeping peacefully.

I can kind of imagine my father with the itch of lust the way I have it. My father whom I stuffed into a taxi today, pulled out of a taxi, walked into his apartment building, pulled in and out of the elevator, led down that deadly quiet hall, white walls, aqua carpet, into his two-room furnished apartment, white walls, aqua carpet, not one picture or plant, refrigerator as bad as Hal Gillette's but three bottles of Johnny Walker Red on the kitchen counter. Walter, once I got you there, I couldn't stay with you a second longer. I know you said you didn't need me to; I know you *did* need me, but I couldn't stay. I hope you understand.

I try opening my mouth and breathing through it, feeling maybe I'll get more air that way. I put my hands flat against my stomach and press, as if I'm holding my insides in. Nothing works.

Jonathan sleeps.

Pricklings of arousal bubble under the anxiety that is the main inhabitant of my body. Anxiety the house, lust the termites. I am falling apart by degrees.

I think: If I didn't know what crazy is, I'd swear I was going crazy now.

Dr. Prewitt, why did you bother getting me well when this world is where I have to take my place? It's too much. I want to reel back the years, past the dolls, past infancy, past gestation: not to kill myself but never to have been born, conceived or conceived of. No parents, no Tabby, no lust. No ridiculous MABEE, no Jonathan, no how to win friends and influence people, how to pick up girls, be your own best friend, be your own worst enemy. Nothing. Simple.

When sperm hits egg, the complications begin, wanting, not getting, hurting and being hurt. Life is suffering, lust is an itch that scratching only worsens; oh, Jon, now all I want to do is make love to you and I don't even like you. No exit.

I have been crouched on the floor near the kids' books, thoughts, feelings, whirling to the fast beat of my heart, the slow of Jon's breath. I stand, then sit, on the room's one chair. I feel something under the seat's cushions.

Aha!

Three copies of *Penthouse* and four paperbacks: *The Pearl, Nights with Alberta, Janice and Her Dirty Tricks, How to Make Love to a Woman.*

> I am an avid reader of letters to Penthouse Forum but I never thought I would have an experience wild enough to prompt my writing such a letter. Recently, however, something happened to change my mind.
>
> My best buddy, Rick, and I were out cruising one night. He is 25 and I am 26 and, I have been told, hung like a horse. This van pulled up next to us at a red light, with these three fine and foxy-looking young ladies, a brunette, a blond, and a redhead. . . .

I sit on the chair in Jonathan's room and I learn the precise dimensions of the letter writer's and his friend's organs ("thick pleasure rods"). I learn exactly how they were placed in each one of the gorgeous girls' several orifices repeatedly and to everyone's satisfaction: in the van, at the beach, and finally at the girls' apartment.

And I am grossed out and I am turned on.

And I sit there in that chair and masturbate while reading that stupid letter while Jonathan sleeps.

The digital clock flips from 3:59 to 4:00. I feel real bad.

Nine

Busted Back Down

HAVING CLIMBED back into bed with the still-sleeping Jonathan, when it was just starting to get light out, I am hardly bright-eyed when Jon's alarm goes off at six. I have not been asleep that early morning, half-dawn quarter-hour in bed with him, only half asleep; but at least I am a little more relaxed, the panic subsiding as reasonlessly as it began. Jon awakens immediately and turns off the alarm. He rolls over and stretches, with a big lascivious smile for me. I notice the gap between his upper two front teeth.

"Hi—iii," he says coyly, stringing it out into two syllables.

"Good morning," I say, unable to smile back at him. We're both lying on our sides, naked, facing each other. I'm just looking, looking, looking at him. The gap between his teeth, the tangled shoulder-length hair, the petulant lower lip, the deep brown eyes and full eyebrows with a few stray scraggly hairs in between at the top of his nose. The color of his skin seems paler, oddly, than it seemed last night. I'm searching for something in his face, but I don't know what.

He takes my scanning of his face as a compliment. "Well," he says smugly, "it *was* pretty good, wasn't it?"

I don't respond. I'm still just looking. I have heard the eyes called "the windows of the soul," but I can't see into Jonathan's soul at all. In some profound way I know as little of Jonathan, Jon now, sixteen-year-old Jon, whom I made love to last night, as I do of Jon the vanished kid whom I never met and never can meet, who once read *Winnie the Pooh* in this same room. And Jon doesn't know me at all. If anyone ever knows anyone else.

Jon puts his hand on my waist and absently strokes up my rib cage toward my armpit, down to the curve of my hip, and back up to my waist, where he rests his hand. With that simple gesture, waves of heat fan up from between my legs. I'm careful not to move or betray this. Torturous. Dangerous.

"Yeah," he says. "I felt like we really entered the one-space last night."

"Entered the one-space?" I ask, unable, or maybe unwilling, to keep the skepticism from my voice. A little voice in me is saying, Oh thank God he didn't come across with this last night!

Jonathan is as insensitive to nuance as my father. "Yeah," he says, resuming that light stroking, "The one-space. It's a spiritual term." By this time I am gummy, squirming inside, consumed by those gentle, casual strokes, drowning, yet still alive enough to bristle with annoyance at his words. How perfect, I think, that he should keep spiritual tracts on his bookshelf, with copies of *Penthouse* hidden below his chair cushion. It is unfair that such a phony can turn me on this authentically.

"I thought it was rather more physical than spiritual,"

I say. My voice sounds strangled to me. Down for the last time. Hello undertow. Out to sea. Glug glug. I let my hand drift down his nice taut stomach and I grasp his prick. Gratifyingly it is fully erect, the skin covering it so oddly soft and velvety.

"Well, well, *well,*" he says, with a jubilant and self-congratulatory smile. "What have we here?"

"Why don't you tell me?" I say, not caring about anything anymore, flushed with heat, wet, distended, grasping, urgent, drowning, "After all . . ." I sound hoarse, "you're the flower and I'm the bud, isn't that right?"

Jonathan's other hand is now doing to me, with great skill, the equivalent of what I'm doing to him. "I wouldn't worry about that if I were you," he says, arrogant, sexy boy. Once again we make love incredibly well. Even my fatigue from being up most of the night seems to add to it; there's not one scrap of resistance or difficulty left in me. I'm so tired I just give in, give in, give in.

When I come out of the shower afterward, Jonathan is sitting on his jute mat, back to the bed, eyes closed, in a lotus position. If I knew where paper and string and a pen and tape were, I think, I could make a little sign and hang it around his neck:

Do Not Disturb:
Meditating

Just as I pretend to Jon that I have no interest in natural foods and vegetarianism because he is so obnoxious about it, I also pretend to him I don't care much about religions, Eastern or otherwise, when in fact I do. Trudy Jurgen's twenty-minute roundup on Buddhism made more sense to me than anything I have ever heard in my life. "Life is suffering." Who could deny it? But then, the other three Noble Truths that Trudy listed on the board, they were the real kickers. The Second Truth was that suffering is caused by desire. And the Third, that desire is caused by attachment. And so, logically enough, comes the Fourth: If you want to end suffering you have to end desire by being detached. One class, a couple of years ago, and I still remember it clearly.

I think about this, watching Jon's smooth, straight, smug pink back and wanting to make love to him yet again. I am about as far from detachment as you can get. I am coated in desire, as thick and sticky as if I had bathed in honey—no wonder suffering sticks to me.

Jon thinks our lovemaking was spiritual? I think it was right out of *Penthouse* Letters to the Editor.

Jonathan and I walk, arm in arm, down the slippery streets of Riverdale to the train station. It is another bitterly cold gray day. When will the weather change? Usually even in winter in New York there are bright, bright brilliantly sunny days now and then. But Jon's mood is unaffected by the weather. He's utterly cheerful, doesn't complain even when I say that I'm not going to MABEE today, doesn't even ask me for an explanation.

Jon's train, into New York, arrives first. I see him off, cross the overpass, and wait for the next train *from* New York, which will take me out to Chilton. I need some time alone.

Ever since I was a little girl I've preferred being alone, reading or playing dolls or going on walks or bicycling or writing, to being with other people. When my mother went back to Rahleigh (She had worked there for years before my brother was born, then she quit to have Steph, went back, quit to have me, then returned to Rahleigh when I was in third grade because my father wasn't making enough money to support us. She has been there ever since.) when she went back she worried that I'd be lonely in the afternoons, feel abandoned. But it was a profound relief to have the house to myself. For, though my father was in the attic writing, he rarely came downstairs, and when he did we did not speak to each other: I had been carefully trained, early on, by my mother, to play "invisible daddy" during Walter's working day.

But though I assured my mother that I was not lonely, that I enjoyed these solitary afternoons, I knew, even then, that she didn't believe me. Even then I knew she sickened herself with something I did not yet have the name for. An infectious disease: soon I felt the same sickening; I felt, obscurely, that there was something bad about enjoying this time alone so greatly. I felt guilty, already a familiar feeling.

All those years ago, Katherine started as a secretary at Rahleigh and Byrd, and now she's a senior editor. Sometimes, I think I'm more proud of her professional achievements than she is.

When I get to Chilton after leaving Riverdale the first thing I do is call my mother at Rahleigh. I always do this if I've spent the night somewhere else. As usual, I'm put right through to her.

"Oh, honey! How nice to hear your voice! I was hoping you would call!"

It tears me up every time, to hear how ecstatic, how delighted my mother sounds at a mere call from me. I don't want to have that big an effect on her—it's too much responsibility.

"Yeah, well, I just thought I'd say hello."

"I was going to call down at MABEE, but I didn't want to interrupt you, that's why I'm so glad you called! An author of mine from Washington who was flying in to see me today is iced in; no planes flying out. So I have lunch free. Would you like to run up and join me?''

She doesn't realize I'm in Chilton. I don't tell her.

''Well, I'd like to, but it would be difficult today. Abby has a dentist's appointment this afternoon and everything got rescheduled because of that; and if I go running off it'll screw up everyone else's schedule.''

''Oh,'' says my mother in a tiny voice. ''I understand.''

I used to think I was this honest, forthright person, a straightforward Sagittarian, but lately I'm getting awfully adept at lying. This disturbs me.

''Maybe tomorrow or Friday?'' I suggest.

''I'm booked up tomorrow and Friday,'' she says, a little petulantly.

''Oh,'' I say. ''Well, then, I guess I'll see you at home.''

''I guess so.'' And then with that little edginess that so often underlies her best trying-to-be-casual tone, she adds, ''Will you be there when I get home tonight?''

''As far as I know.''

''What does *that* mean?''

''It means as far as I know, Katherine. As far as I know, unless my plans change in some unforeseeable way, yes, I'll be here, I mean there!''

''If your plans change, will you notify me?''

''Yes.''

It is no use saying, ''Haven't I consistently kept you apprised of my whereabouts since I got into vitamin therapy and out of Grace?'' I remind myself for the two millionth time, *Elizabeth, you did this to her. You made her this way, you fanned the coals till they glowed and made her walk them; your hospitalization ate up her forty-eight-thousand-dollar inheritance that she could have quit Rahleigh on and written her novel with instead of having to play office politics with Phil Heindorf and nurse along authors like Cam Peckinpaker. You did this to her. So, Elizabeth, you can goddamn well try to be kind and patient and try to be there for her, because without you she wouldn't need someone to be there for her as desperately as she does now.*

But I wonder if any amount of kindness and patience on my part will ever be enough to stanch her fear and loneliness.

My mother has a recurring nightmare about me.

My parents probably wouldn't even be getting a divorce if it weren't for me.

Though, I remind myself, they would have needed one in any case. My "illness," as Katherine sometimes puts it, just brought the problems they'd always had to the fore.

"Yes, Katherine, I'll let you know if anything changes, but I'm sure it won't. And, listen, I didn't mean I was trying to change my plans, or waiting for a better offer, or waiting for someone to call me back or something. It's just a phrase, you know, 'as far as I know.' "

"Well, it just leaves me hanging." Under her surface huffiness, I feel her fear. I'm so tired of her fear!

"I'm sorry. I didn't mean to leave you hanging. It's just, I was going to call Dr. Prewitt for an appointment and if this afternoon is the only time I can see her . . ."

"Why do you need to see Dr. Prewitt, is something wrong?" Panic and fear, now overt, scrape her voice. "Are you all right, Elizabeth?"

"Yes yes yes, I'm all right, Katherine, I'm fine! I just wanted to . . ." Talk to her about that anxiety last night is what I want to do, but this is not something I can say to my mother without making *her* unbearably anxious. In a brilliant, deceptive, creative flash I say, " . . . to see how long I have to stay on the vitamins. It's not easy taking so many pills, and you know, I'm feeling so good these days that I was just wondering if . . ."

My mother's relief is audible. "Now, Elizabeth, don't you *dare* stop taking those vitamins unless Dr. Prewitt tells you it's okay, do you understand?" She sounds positively cheerful, delivering this warm, mild, maternal scolding.

Playing to this, I say, "Well, I thought I could maybe just reduce the number of vitamins . . ."

"Elizabeth! If, and only if, and not before, Dr. Prewitt says so. All right? Promise me?"

"I promise."

"Look, call me back if you are seeing her today, okay?"

"Okay."

"By the way, Elizabeth, a letter came for you from Tabitha. It'll be waiting for you on the dining-room table when you get home."

After I read the letter from Tabby, I run a hot bath for myself even though it's the middle of the day and I just showered at Jon's a few hours before. I am so tired. As the tub fills I heat a little olive oil downstairs, then rub it into my hair and tie my hair back under a kerchief. I mix up a facial mask consisting of an egg white, a teaspoon of honey, and a little bit of oatmeal. I spread this on my face to dry out for ten minutes while I sit on the toilet with its lid down reading *Esquire* magazine (my father's magazine subscriptions still come here), waiting for the tub to fill. As it dries, the mask makes my face tight. When I pull my lips back into a smile it feels as if my cheeks will shatter: I imagine this is the way my mother feels, smiling at Phil Heindorf and Camille Blanche Peckinpaker and the hundreds of others she meets and works with, who ''swirl and swirl,'' who are ''too complicated to go into'' with me.

In the bath, scrubbing off the dried egg white, shampooing out the olive oil, I think about how I routinely do these beauty things like facials and how, though I enjoy doing them, I don't think they make one rat's-ass worth of difference in how I look. Now makeup does make a difference. It does make me prettier, ''plays up,'' as the fashion magazines say, my big eyes, ''tones down,'' with careful shading, my big nose. But I'm not sure I *like* the prettier that makeup makes me. It looks good but phony. A lot of times, in the Merle Norman ads, I like the Befores much better than the Afters. Even though the Afters are prettier, I feel that I would like the Befores better as people. I float back and forth on makeup. I haven't worn any in the past month or so, but I haven't thrown out what I have. Because for sure even when I don't like my cooked, finished, polished, pretty-pretty face at the end, I always have fun putting makeup on. Stroking my eyelashes with mascara, puffing on powder blush with the little soft brush—concentrating fully on this oval of face, big-nosed, big-eyed; mine, me, yet standing in front of the mirror I'm looking at it abstractly as if it wasn't me, while I gently, neutrally, pat and rub and stroke and line and blot colors in tubes and pots and sticks and crayons and jars and bottles.

Of course, since my underlying beef about makeup is that I think it's dishonest, maybe I ought to wear it these days, given how many lies I find myself telling.

In the bath, I hear myself sigh. I realize what's prompted this sigh: *Oh, Elizabeth, can't you do one simple thing, like put on makeup or not put on makeup, without having complicated feelings about it?*

I wonder if without realizing it I sigh as often and as deeply as my mother.

After my bath, I realize I haven't eaten yet. It's now around one o'clock. I have some cheese melted on a piece of bread, an apple, some potato chips, a Diet Pepsi, a dish of Häagen-Dazs chocolate-chocolate chip ice cream, and two cinnamon graham crackers. I am so tired.

I call Dr. Prewitt's office to set up an appointment. It happens that there has just been a cancellation tomorrow afternoon, Thursday. Would that be convenient for me? That would be convenient for me.

Then I call my father. He says he's fine. His next shock treatment is on Friday, a week from tomorrow. Could I pick him up afterward, same time, same place? Saul is still out of town, Paul is still in the hospital, he is not seeing Kris all that seriously, and under the circumstances he really can't ask Katherine. . . .

Sure.

After I hang up, I try to imagine my father, instead of implying that he needs me to come and get him because he can't get anyone else, I am the last on the list but the only one available, saying something like, "Even though we've had our ups and downs, Elizabeth, I love you and I know you love me, so I want *you* to be the one to pick me up." Or "Because you've just gone through such a difficult period, and because you also write, I feel you can understand me and what I'm going through. And I *need* someone who understands me, who loves me, to help me."

But I can't imagine my father saying this any more than I can imagine my saying, "I can't deal with this, Walter, get someone else to pick you up" or "Pull your socks up, Walter!"

* * *

Next I call Hal Gillette, who is very happy to hear from me. That's his exact phrase. "I'm very happy to hear from you, Elizabeth! I was afraid you had just dropped off the edge of the earth!"

"Not quite," I say. Although sex with Jonathan was pretty close.

"Well, would you like to get together? I'm thinking about going to this poetry reading next Friday. I thought, since you write, maybe you'd like to come?"

Next Friday . . . I will have just taken Walter home from his shock treatment. I'll need something.

I ask Hal Gillette who it is that's reading. It's someone I've never heard of but he says is pretty famous, a feminist poet of some repute, Gina something.

Hal Gillette is so unguarded. I think he is the most unguarded person I have ever met. He's another adult I feel older than. He still reminds me of mashed potatoes. He also reminds me of a puppy. He also protects me by being neutral, not really knowing me, not being someone I have strong feelings about. He especially protects me now that I'm, to use a Tabby phrase, "in lust" with Jonathan.

"Sure, Hal," I say. "Love to."

I go up to my room and sleep for a couple of hours. When I wake up it's four-thirty and, since it's November, already dark. I wake up suddenly, panicked again, and disoriented at first. But it's not as bad as last night. I force myself to get out of bed and breathe deeply. I walk around the strange, familiar house, my mother's house, turning on lights and pulling down shades. I set the table. I don't know what my mother has planned for dinner but I'm sure baked potatoes wouldn't be amiss. I scrub two and put them in the oven at 375°. I build a fire in the fireplace, knowing that will also please my mother.

And I reread Tabby's letter.

> Busted back down to locked single room, Lizzie-Liz, very freaky, going down fast, feel so bad.
>
> Love ya, Always,
> Tab

I get a clipboard and a pen and some lined paper; I plan to write a rough draft and then recopy it. This letter must be without mistakes, skipped words, misspellings, non sequiturs. Perfect. Sane. Sitting by the fire I begin.

> Dear Mr. and Mrs. Whittaker:
>
> How are you? I guess you heard from Tabitha that I got expelled from Lakeland too, right before she did. But I am fine now, I really am, because—and I know that you may not believe this—of vitamin therapy

> Dear Mr. and Mrs. Whittaker:
>
> I am writing on behalf of megavitamin therapy for Tabby.

> Dear Mr. and Mrs. Whittaker:
>
> ~~About two weeks after Tabitha~~
>
> I guess you know that I was expelled from Lakeland just before Tabitha got ~~caught screwing Paul Viguerie in the boys' dorm~~ expelled. She may have also told you that after that I made another suicide attempt, much more serious than the two at Lakeland. I nearly died. After it, I was hospitalized at two different mental hospitals, one of them here in New York. Well, at the second hospital, I got put on a new kind of therapy, which

involves taking large doses of vitamins, and let me tell you

Dear Mr. and Mrs. Whittaker:

I don't know how I can convince you, but I feel I must try. It is very very important to take Tabitha out of Twelvetrees and put her somewhere where she can go on vitamin therapy. I know, from the conversations she and I used to have at Lakeland, that we had very similar problems. Vitamin therapy has helped me a lot, and I know it can help her. It is safe and harmless, too. I didn't believe in it either, but it didn't matter what I believed; after I took the megavitamins for a couple of months they worked. I changed. It is hard for me to say this, but I used to hear voices calling me, and now I don't. And food, which had started tasting metallic to me, began to taste good again. Also, just like Tabitha, I got very depressed at times. I no longer have that. I haven't even thought of suicide in months ~~despite the fact that~~

Dear Mr. and Mrs. Whittaker:

I know you probably think I am the last person in the world to give advice about therapy or anything else, but I have to tell you how much vitamin therapy helped me and that I think it could help Tabitha, too. Despite the fact that my whole family is falling apart—my father is starting shock treatments and he and my mother are probably getting divorced—I am handling everything very well and have not thought of suicide even once!

Dear Mr. and Mrs. Whittaker:

You and Tabitha's therapist are not the only ones who don't believe in megavitamin therapy. I didn't either. ~~It saved me, though for what I don't know~~

Dear Mr. and Mrs. Whittaker:

I urge you to get Tabitha onto vitamin therapy quickly, before it is too late for her.

I pull the sheet of paper from the clipboard, crumple it into a ball, and throw it into the fire. I reread Tabby's letter, then I ball it up, too, and toss it. I think about her underlining the word "always." I sit there by the fire, watching the flames that have consumed my words and Tabby's words, and I wait for my mother to get home.

Ten

If Lost Please Return To

I KNOW what my mother's recurring dream about me is.

She sees me walking toward her, coming down a hill. My father stands beside her. Behind me is a skyline, buildings in geometric bites against the sky.

Then my mother realizes that what she thought were distant skyscrapers are tombstones, silhouetted at the top of the hill, not far away at all.

But I am walking away from the graves, down the hill, toward her. I will be safe, she thinks.

Then my father starts yelling angrily to me, "Pull your socks up, Elizabeth! Just pull your damn socks up!"

My mother looks at my feet, and sure enough, the knee socks I am wearing in her dream have tumbled down and are baggily wrinkled around my ankles.

It is only then she notices that my legs, from ankle to knee, are skeletons.

I was expelled from Lakeland for my second suicide attempt, the one where Tabby found me, the one where Trudy Jurgen drove me in the school van to Lake County

General where first they sponged off the razor cuts (they were not very deep) with alcohol and Trudy asked me, as I lay on the table, "Does it sting?"; and when I nodded yes, replied, "Good, I hope it does; you have been a very foolish girl." And then an annoyed-looking intern said, "All right, we're going to put this tube down your nose, it's not pleasant, please *try to swallow, relax and try to swallow, try to swallow,"* and then I fell out into black nothingness, though when I first woke up from it I sensed I had been there, somewhere, all along, only I could not remember where. My bandaged arms stung, my throat and nose burned, I was very thirsty, and I felt: oh no, oh no no no no no no. I had started, again, to leave but had lacked nerve. I had not finished the job. Now the consequences of my failed act would cave in on me like beams and rafters falling in a burning building. I felt pain of such magnitude, my own and what my parents' would be; I felt a crushing lack of alternatives, choices, chances. I felt utterly without hope. I had done it now, irrevocably; now I would be expelled from Lakeland; now I would be returned to Chilton and to my troubled parents; now I would be separated from Tabby, from the sort-of social life I had at school. . . .

So why didn't you think of all that before, Elizabeth?

Because I couldn't think.

Because even while on a relative scale I "enjoyed" Lakeland much better than I did Chilton, I was in a realm so far from "enjoyment," "thinking," "choosing," "deciding" most of the time that it defied my capacity to put it into words then or now; only—and I understand, Trudy, why it looked to you like a fifteen-year-old's histrionics and I don't blame you for your inaccurate assessment, though I do blame Phipps—only *it was unbearable.* When that, whatever it was, happened, the world closed down to a small, unbearable point from which there was no exit and time slowed to the torturous drip of the sink with the very slow leak across the hall from Tabby's and my room.

Drip.

Drip.

Drip.

I . . . should . . . get up . . . turn . . . the faucet . . . tighter . . . and . . . I'm thirsty . . . but what . . . it will take . . . to sit . . . up . . . to swing . . . my legs . . . over the bed . . . my knees . . . will . . . have to bend . . . my feet . . . rest on the floor . . . my body . . . propelled now . . . to rise . . . one foot . . . will have to . . . swing out . . . in front of the other . . . alternately . . . the feet taking turns . . . the balance must shift . . . it is called "walking" . . . to get a glass, the eyes . . . must scan . . . the brain . . . coordinate . . . the feet . . . legs . . . body . . . fingers must unfurl . . . to hold the glass . . . then close back . . . around it. . . .

No I
think
I will
stay
here
in
bed.

When I woke up in the hospital at Lakeland, so weighed down by pain and hopelessness that I could not bear to be conscious, could not open my eyes, I was terribly thirsty.

I felt someone put a straw between my lips. Reflexively, I sucked.

An icy, thick vanilla ice-cream shake flowed into my mouth and down my bruised throat, cool and sweet and soothing, absolutely, incredibly delicious. Nothing had ever tasted so good in my life as that cold, thick vanilla shake. Sucking that straw was all that mattered.

After a while I opened my eyes. I looked down the straw to the large paper cup to the hand holding it: delicate fingers; skin around the small knuckles slightly freckled; simple wedding band; unpainted, not-too-long nails, carefully filed into neat ovals. I followed the hand up the arm to the shoulder and face of my mother. The intensity of the gaze upon her face, the power and strength in her eyes *willing* me to live was matched only by the depths of sorrow I saw there. It was a look that will stay with me forever.

I shut my eyes again.

When people say, "I wish I had your mother," they don't know the tiniest portion of Katherine's love and strength and power and pain.

But they also don't know the price exacted.

As I walk, now, to Dr. Prewitt's office, I think of that mysterious, terrifying, and incommunicable time. It occurs to me that I still find life, my life, close to unbearable. I sometimes feel that I am walking around without a skin: when I pass a Moonie selling roses on the corner of Lex and Twenty-third my eyes fill automatically. Because he is not much older than me, because he is not wearing gloves, because I cannot imagine what led him to be here, selling roses in the bitter cold.

I know, too, no matter how much the shrinks say, like Sid, "You *choose* thus-and-such," that some actions that appear to be choices or decisions *are not*. I wish like hell everything was choice, but that is cruel, unrealistic and supremely self-motivated; if everything's choice, then we never have to help each other. Did that Moonie "choose" to be there? Did I "choose" to have a chemical imbalance?

But there are some things I *have* chosen. I choose, for

instance to stay at MABEE, though I hate it, until I can find some other place to be. I choose to be there, and to omit the details of what the place is really like, for my parents' sake, particularly Katherine's, because I can see how that earlier period, the period *not* of my choosing, of the chemical imbalance and all the consequences that metastasized from that, caused them such deep pain that they may never recover. But when I find someplace else, I will choose to leave MABEE. And I will recover. I think. I hope. And then, whether or not they, my parents, recover, it will be up to them, a matter of their own choosing; it will not be because of what their daughter did.

I will not live my life as if acted upon. I will not be a victim. I will not be like Katherine.

But neither will I believe, like Sid Meyerhoff, that everything is a matter of choice.

I say to the Moonie, "No, thanks," in reply to his hopeful, "Fresh roses?" He gives me this big, vacant smile they all have. Tears sting in my eyes as I walk past, because I know, from my own experience, that those very things which lead people to seemingly make choices or decisions are sometimes so terrible that no one, no one, outside of the person himself, can grasp the magnitude. And sometimes, maybe often, not even the person himself.

I think about that Tibetan poster on Jonathan's wall, which is like the circles within the circles within the circles that I have thought about. Each circle with its tiny gods and goddesses, devils and demons, snarling dogs, yawning lions, angels with wings spread; how odd that some ancient Tibetan could come so close to drawing what is the closest thing to a map, or model, of the world that I have. Problems in problems in problems.

But what I want to know is what's in the center of the

very, very innermost circle? What is the core, the seed, the nucleus, around which all the problems form? If you took away all the problems, what would be left?

But if life still seems to me unbearable, if almost any time I look someone directly in the eyes I feel like crying (unless that someone is a lover, in which case I feel a screen come down)—why, then, do I not again try to kill myself?

Dr. Prewitt, a tall, big-boned woman, heavy but so tall that she carries it well, is unique in shrinkdom. She has never once talked to me about my problems or asked about my family (though she has met them). She simply gave me that questionnaire to fill out, went over the answers when I was done, and told us—my parents separately from me—that she thought I could benefit from vitamin therapy. She prescribed the dosage, which I would take at Grace Memorial for three weeks and then continue at home for another year, after which I might well no longer need the pills, the problem—which had to do with the way my body metabolized adrenaline—then having been cured.

To me, she said simply, clearly, directly, looking straight at me through her octagonal tortoiseshell glasses, "Schizophrenia is a physical disease with emotional and mental symptoms. Often, with persons who have a disposition toward it, the onset is in the early or midteens; and having caught it so early we can have every anticipation of a complete cure. The vitamins, which you will not have to take forever, will cure the perceptual changes. Within three months, Elizabeth, I give you my word that you will no longer hear voices, food will no longer taste peculiar, and any changes in mood you experience will be based on real, actual occurrences, understandable to you. You will not suffer from deep, uncontrollable depressions anymore. Do you understand?''

It was one of my better days, so I could say, ''Yes, I understand,'' and add, ''I don't believe in it, though.''

Dr. Prewitt smiled. ''Fortunately,'' she said, ''you don't have to believe in it for it to work.''

Within three months, what she had said would happen, happened.

Because I had planned to walk from MABEE to Dr. Prewitt's office after school today, I brought warm clothes in from Chilton this morning: my down jacket, leg warmers, my low-heeled rubber-bottomed boots with the fake-fur lining, and wool pants and several sweaters. It is a walk of nineteen blocks to Dr. Prewitt's and I am hoping that this cold walk will have the effect on me that cold showers are supposed to have, i.e., knock out excessive and continual sexual arousal. Since night before last, with Jon, I have been in a state. Just the sight of Jon at school today turned my legs into overcooked pasta. Of course I tried to act cool, but this silly asinine grin keeps floating across my face whenever I look at Jon. Our usual early-morning quickie make-out session in the common room devastated me. He wants me to call him tonight after I get through with Dr. Prewitt. I don't know; maybe I will, maybe I won't.

If only I *liked* him it would be much simpler.

It is unbelievably cold out; the wind cuts through my coat as if it was nothing. I walk briskly, willing myself not to shiver because that only makes you colder. I *refuse* to give up and take a bus or a cab; I said I was going to walk, I'll walk.

It is depressingly gray again today. I try to remember the last time it was sunny. I know this can't be right, but the last day I remember was the afternoon I first really talked to Harvey, back after I got expelled from Lakeland. I used to come into the city often, blue blue blue and scared that THAT would happen again. I was seeing a shrink, a Dr. Gold whose office was way, way east on the second story of a brownstone building across the street from the mayor's mansion and the East River. I didn't like Dr. Gold at all; he was of the school that doesn't ask questions—the patient is supposed to just sit there and blurt out whatever's on their mind, and I couldn't.

He put me on a drug described to me as a "mood elevator," but it did not seem to have any effect on me. I was to take two pills three times a day. They were small, bright pink pills with the drug company's name in white letters on them; they were shaped like miniature M&M's.

Often I sat in Dr. Gold's office and just cried quietly. My appointment was in the late afternoon in that weird, sad, dusky half-lit time of day. His office was in muted gray-green tones, somber; there was a wall of built-in book shelves, book-filled, behind him. He did not put on a lamp until it was fully dark.

If I wasn't crying silently, I was looking out the window into the tree branches, watching the squirrels perform acrobatic leaps. Concentrating on the squirrels helped me not cry, not think about the fact that I knew down to my bones that Dr. Gold was not helping me in any way and that his method could never help me. I knew, too, that my parents could ill afford the eighty dollars an hour ticked away in that office, ticked as slowly as the drips in the Lakeland sink, while the squirrels leaped and chittered.

Because I saw Dr. Gold three times a week I was in the city a lot, and even on my non-Dr.-Gold days I'd often commute in just to *not* be in Chilton. I'd wander around; I'd have a cup of coffee or a glass of orange juice at a cafe and spin it out into an hour of sitting, staring out at people or perhaps reading a paperback book. I went to museums, I sat in parks, I browsed at bookstores. I discovered that just above the elevators which connect Grand Central to the Pan Am Building there was a little balustraded overlook, from which I could see all of the huge main lobby of Grand Central, thousands of people at times, near deserted at others; people scurrying this way and that, antlike, busy but inconsequential under the vast, vaulted ceilings.

Through all this, I heard the voices on and off. Sometimes they'd call my name; sometimes they'd murmur softly for hours; but I could never quite make out what they were saying. When food tasted normal, I'd eat; when it didn't, I wouldn't. Sweets were the only thing that could be depended on not to taste coppery, metallic, bitter, tainted.

I went to movies sometimes.

It was at a movie theater on East Eighth Street, where *The Big Heat*, a fifties gangster movie in ominous black and white, was playing, that I first talked to Harvey. That particular theater had an odd, shabby-elegant lobby, with black and white marble tiles on the floor and a little coffee-and-dessert bar. Between *The Big Heat* and the second feature, *This Gun for Hire*, I had a cup of coffee and a brownie. Though all the other stools at the counter were empty, a slight, very pale man, blond, with wire-rim glasses, sat down next to me.

"So, what'd you think?" he asked me. He did not smile, and he was too unhealthy looking to be attractive, but his manner was self-assured.

"It seemed unfair to me," I said, "that just as Gloria Grahame was getting straightened out she got that coffee thrown in her face."

He laughed soundlessly. "Don't you know *anything* about movies of this period?" he asked. "Sin, suffer, repent. She had to suffer more than just the pangs of her conscience before she could be transformed from a gangster's moll into a good girl." He tipped his head to one side and contemplated me. "Are *you* a good girl?" he asked me.

The odd thing is, I can't remember what I answered. That was Harvey. We sat together for *This Gun for Hire.*

The sunny day which is the last I can remember in months was a week or two later, when, coincidentally, I met Harvey again. I was in the city. It was a non-Dr.-Gold day, so I had just been wandering around. I wound up at Washington Square Park, sitting on a bench, looking out toward the fountain, deeply sad. There were no voices that day, just the bottomless sinking depression.

And Harvey came by.

He stopped in front of me. He did not seem at all surprised to see me. "Well, Elizabeth," he said, still unsmiling. I went home with him. I didn't call my parents. We went to sleep about five A.M., when gray morning light was just beginning to wash into his tiny, dirty bedroom. We didn't get up till around sundown the next day, which was when I had that fluke orgasm. But the third day, or maybe it was the fourth, or maybe it was night, food began to taste unpleasant, and so I stopped eating. When Harvey went out for Chinese food I stayed on his narrow unmade bed, very slowly counting the bricks in the apartment's one exposed brick wall until I got to twenty-nine and couldn't remember what number came next; and, anyway, it didn't matter because I was getting numb myself, then more numb. . . .

When Harvey came back—it was two in the morning—he said, "Hey, Elizabeth, it's been cool having you here, but tomorrow you need to split, okay?" He was rolling a joint, looking down at the white paper and the dried, crumpled green marijuana on his kitchen table as he spoke.

"Okay."

I felt, distinctly, that there was no place on earth to which I could go.

It was very complicated, getting to the bathroom, taking off the cap, but the pink pills, being small and coated, went down easily.

"I'm . . . going . . . to . . . bed . . ."

"You want some of this?" he waved the joint at me.

I shook my head.

"Unh-unnh." Ohhhhh . . . so tired. Just to . . .

Sleep.

"Elizabeth! What's this!"

He's woken me up. He's shaking me.

Man, just let me *sleep*.

"Elizabeth! I found this in the bathroom! Goddamnit, were these yours? What did you take? What did you take, how many? How could you! Jesus Christ . . ."

The last thing I remember was Harvey propping me against the doorframe, pulling my hair, and slapping me. It didn't work. I gave in to that delicious undertow, *so* sleepy I didn't care anymore, just let me sleep.

Later I learned I was taken to Bellevue, the nearest hospital.

Harvey did not know my last name. He did not know my parents' names or address. He did not know I was sixteen.

The notebook I carried around with me in my purse, even then, is what saved me. In the upper-right-hand corner of the first page I had written IF LOST PLEASE RETURN TO and my name and address. That's how they found my parents.

I never saw Harvey again.

* * *

Later I learned that "mood elevators" are among the most potentially lethal of all drugs. They have no antidote. Once in the bloodstream, there is nothing much that can be done. My stomach was pumped. I was put on a kidney machine. I slept through all this. I slept through my parents' arrival, at six that morning, through my father telling my mother, "I can't handle this," and leaving her alone while he went off to stay with friends on Cape Cod. I slept for four days.

When I could be moved, I was transferred to another hospital. At the moment when they lifted the stretcher into the ambulance, I awoke for a second to see a padded blue-foam surface with little holes come close to my face, then recede. The ceiling of the ambulance. I turned my head to one side and met the gaze of my mother, her eyes so incredibly green, her whole being pointed toward me like a compass needle pointing to north, automatic, quivering and steady at the same time. Like at Lakeland with the milk shake, only more so.

I closed my eyes a second time.

From the second hospital I was transferred to Hurstview, in upstate New York. The car ride up there is when I remember the rain starting, sheets of gray rain surrounding us in the car, enclosing us. My father, who had reappeared by then, driving; my mother next to him in front, face drawn; me in back, tears rolling down my face. Only the windshield wipers gliding rhythmically back and forth. No one spoke. I cried silently the entire time.

As we pulled up to the locked iron gate, affixed to two large, square, gray stone pillars, I burst out, "Please, please don't put me here. Please. I'll never do it again. *Please* don't lock me up!"

My mother said gently, sadly, "We have no choice, honey. Even if we wanted to, according to New York state law you have to have fifteen days' observation after a suicide attempt. Please, honey, please try to cooperate, try to understand."

My father growled, "You got yourself into this, Elizabeth, you can goddamn well face up to the consequences."

"Oh, *Walter!*" said my mother. I saw her face contract in pain as if she'd been hit; I saw her bite her lip and turn away, press her face against the glass.

My father got out into the pouring rain to press a buzzer on the pillar to the left of the gate. In a few moments a male attendant drove down to the gate in a small, tidy silver Toyota. He ran out, opened the gate, and came to our car. I was to get into his car. My parents were to follow.

When I entered the Toyota, my face and hair wet, the attendant turned to me and said, "And how are *we* today, Elizabeth?"

Hurstview, where the psychiatrist told me "If you work you can be out by the time you're twenty or twenty-five," was also where I was given so many tranquilizers that the period is a blur. I do remember sitting by the window watching the rain fall into the gardens. I do remember the red, red Hawaiian Punch we were given to take our medication with, and the green, green walls, and an older, disoriented, unshaven man who stumbled up and down the halls and who I knew somehow was an alcoholic drying out. And I guess, now that I think of it, there was at least one sunny day, for once I was walked down a long, long, long green hall to a pool for recreational swimming. I don't remember whether I went in the water or not, but I do know the sun hurt my eyes and that in the evening my back broke out in hundreds of tiny stingy-itchy little blisters.

"Some patients on your medication do not tolerate sun," a nurse told me.

I was taken off swim privileges, left on medication.

Two weeks later a nurse came in to help me pack. "You're being moved to another wing!" she told me, in tones of cheery congratulation.

"I am?"

"Unh-hunh," she said. "You must have been a good girl, Elizabeth!"

Half an hour later, my parents arrived. The fifteen days were up. They were taking me out. Right through the fog of Thorazine, the fog that eliminated the voices because it eliminated everything, I was overjoyed—but only until they told me they were putting me somewhere else.

"Where?"

"It's in New York, Grace Memorial," said my mother. "And you'll be off tranquilizers. We're going to try something new, vitamin therapy."

I've always wondered why the nurse at Hurstview lied to me and told me I was being moved to another wing. I know that's the kind of stuff Tabby must have to deal with every day at Twelvetrees now.

By now, these thoughts have taken me nineteen blocks through the cold to Dr. Prewitt's building. In the warm lobby I remove my gloves, rub my chilled face. I walk to the bank of elevators. The elevator arrives. I step in. I think about how random it is.

Only five months ago, I was put on vitamin therapy.

The way my parents heard about vitamin therapy was that my father happened to hear Linus Pauling on Dick

Cavett, speaking about the nutritional approach to mental illness.

It could so easily have not happened.

In the car, going from Hurstview to Grace Memorial, the tranquilizers begin to wear off. I burst into angry laughter. "Vitamin therapy! You must be kidding! Look, I may be crazy, but what the hell do *vitamins* have to do with it?"

My mother said, "Well, we'll just try it."

My father said, "You will *take* those goddamn vitamins and you will *shut up* and we will *make* this drive in *peace*, do you understand? You are *making me crazy!*"

Part of vitamin therapy was I wasn't supposed to eat refined foods or sugar while in the hospital. There was a kitchen on the ward, though, where patients might have snacks. Always on hand were white bread and strawberry jam. One night I made some toast for myself. I was just spreading jam on it when this large black nurse (nice in the sense that she did not seem to treat inmates as noticeably mentally ill) showed up. We were talking about her grandchildren, when suddenly what I was eating registered.

"Wait a minute," she said. "Ain't you Dr. Prewitt's patient? You not s'posed to be eatin' that."

"Oh, come on," I said soothingly. "Look, I may be crazy, but what on earth could what I *eat* have to do with it? If eating toast made you crazy, then *everybody* would be locked up!"

She thought about it. "You right," she finally said.

Later on, when Adele (who used to go to MABEE) and I compared notes about Grace Memorial, this nurse was one we both remembered.

* * *

My mother had told me, "When he left me at Bellevue that morning with you still unconscious and went off to Cape Cod, I knew the marriage had to end."

It was late April when I was in Bellevue, May when I was in Hurstview, end of May and beginning of June when I was in Grace Memorial. The end of July, Walter moved out. Katherine started trying to get me into schools, and we lived together that dreadful, fragile rainy summer, tiptoeing around each other; around my gradual improvement and her fear, no less intense than mine but equally unstated, that I would go crazy again; around Walter's absence, around her loneliness, around the office politics at Rahleigh and Byrd which began to fill her conversations and silences which had once been filled with discussions of authors and books. At that same time, my Uncle Jay, who had been seriously ill for years, began the final business of dying. He went into the hospital one more time, the last stop on his journey toward death, and Katherine spent as much time there as she could with Pat. Every day she looked stretched thinner and thinner. In the house at Chilton, I was alone much of the time, grateful to be away from Katherine, guilty at that gratitude, sad yet unconnected emotionally to the end of Jay's life at the hospital in New York. I wanted to be able to feel again, to be compassionate and helpful to my aunt and mother, but I was too absorbed in and confused by my own situation to begin to do that. Every day the voices grew less; I'd hear them perhaps only once or twice, and they'd fade out, fainter. And then they simply stopped. It was gradual enough so that several days passed before I noticed that they weren't there. At that point I began to seriously observe myself, measure my condition as if I were myself an orderly in a hospital; and what I observed was that another gradual change was taking place, the violent thunderstorms of feeling were giving way to—to what? That I didn't know. Certainly not to happiness, for I felt sad most of the time, confused about what had happened to me and to my family and utterly at a loss as to what I would do in the future. And yet, I was "better"; this strange no-man's-land of not being mentally ill yet not having a place in the world, this endless sadness, yes, this was "better." But what next?

I read. I wandered around in the house. I went on walks in the rain—warm summer rain, gray summer skies, mud and puddles on the path—along Edgers Lane, Emmett's Field, the old Zinsser estate, the places I had walked forever, the places I could remember walking as a little girl in a red coat and hat, hand in mittened hand with my mother, Chilton the same, but I and everything in my world so utterly changed. Back home in the quiet house, the rain falling comfortingly on the roof, I'd dry my hair with a towel, being careful to hang it back up so Katherine wouldn't have to walk into a messy house after a long day at the hospital and at Rahleigh. I heated up Campbell's soup, I made sandwiches for myself. When it rang, I answered the telephone. It was generally one of two people. Sometimes it was Walter. "Yes, I'm fine," I'd say. "Just fine. And you?" He'd say he was fine, too. He'd ask if he could talk to Katherine. "She's not here," I'd say. "She's at the hospital with Pat." "Oh, right," Walter would say. "Right, right."

More often it was Katherine who called. "Yes, I'm fine. No, really, I am. But how are *you?*" "Ohhhh . . . okay I guess . . ." a pause, then ". . . but tell me about you, what did you have to eat?"

"Let's see, I had a cheese and tomato sandwich. No, open-faced, under the broiler. On rye bread. Katherine, how's Jay? How's Pat?"

"The same, the same, Pat's not getting enough sleep, Jay looks terrible. . . . Elizabeth, *really*, how are you, are you sure you're not lonely?"

"No no no I'm not lonely. I've got something good to read, Salinger. No, *Raise High the Roof Beam, Carpenters.* And then there's an old Bette Davis movie on Channel 9. I know you have to be there, it's okay. I'm fine. It's okay!" For God's sake, Katherine, it's okay, I'm fine, Jay's dying. You need to be there, I know, and it is a relief for me to be here alone, as it was when you went back to Rahleigh and Byrd when I was in fourth grade, as I can never, never tell you but as I feel so fervently.

So. That was July, that was August.

Schools kept turning me down. They didn't even want to interview me.

In late August, Katherine heard about MABEE.

In September, I started there.

And now it is November, late November, and I am going to see Dr. Prewitt.

I tell her about Jonathan. I tell her about the anxiety. "Is that supposed to happen?" I ask.

She half smiles. "Supposed to? Elizabeth, there is no single path that all people on vitamin therapy are supposed to follow, with *x, y, z* happening at a particular time, any more than there is for people *not* on vitamin therapy."

"So it's *not* supposed to happen?"

"It's not a question of whether or not it's supposed to, Elizabeth, it *did* happen. To you. And in your case, I would say it sounds to me like a hopeful sign. You are back in the world of feelings, feelings that, though they may be painful, have a cause. The ice is melting."

"But I felt it didn't have a cause." My words sound

whiny to me, but they are slow and cumbersome, far from what I am feeling and beginning to form into thoughts. The ice . . . melting. Something good about feeling so bad. What if that seemingly reasonless terror not only had a reason but was the beginning of something new for me?

Because something new would have to be better than what has been so far.

Wouldn't it?

But Dr. Prewitt, not in on these leaps of thought, responds to my statement, whiny or not, "I think, from what you've told me, it did have a very definite cause. The strange house, the very exciting lovemaking with the boy you don't completely care for . . . but. Whatever the cause may or not be, you know the only mode of therapy I am working with these days is vitamins, and I hope you will forgive me if I say I cannot talk with you more about the particulars of your life. I simply feel compelled to reach out to those who are as sad and lost as you were when your parents first brought you here last summer. But if you do want to work with a more conventional therapist at this point as well, I can give you the names of some excellent ones."

"No," I say. "I've already seen too many of them."

"That makes sense to me," she says, nodding slightly. "Considering what you've been through, Elizabeth. It often seems to me that my young patients, like you, have such incredible resilience and courage to come through the pain of these terrible misdiagnoses." She shakes her head. "I have a great deal of respect for you."

"But what else could I have done but go through it?"

"You could have given up."

"I tried."

"Yes, I know, but you also fought back. You really

wrestled with a powerful, baffling disease that most people in the world still don't understand in the least. And you won."

"But I haven't won. I still feel confused, my life is in a mess. . . ."

"And here you are, trying to do something about it. Believing that perhaps it is possible."

Believing that perhaps it is possible.

But still I question her. "If I won, Dr. Prewitt, why did I feel that way the other night?"

"Well, I've already said your feelings make perfect, rational sense to me given the situation. But let me ask you a question. Did you ever have an anxiety attack like that before you began megavitamin therapy?"

I think back through the years and finally shake my head. Whatever the range of my symptoms, they have never, never included anything like that sleepless, terrifying night at Jonathan's.

"I didn't think so; they're not part of this kind of schizophrenia per se." She stares thoughtfully for a moment at a pottery jug of deep wine-red carnations on her desk, then looks back at me. "You see, once the schizophrenia as such has been treated, the patient is still left with his or her world to deal with, good, bad, or indifferent. You understand?"

I love listening to her, not only because of what she says but the way she says it. There is just the faintest trace of a foreign accent—I don't know which one—in her speech, and her idiom is just slightly exotic. I feel as if her words massage me. If she were doing regular therapy, she is one person I would not mind having it with. But perhaps part of what I like about her is knowing that she's not, that she won't, that she doesn't. It makes me feel that she responds to me as a person, not exactly as a friend—but not a shrink, counselor, therapist, psychologist, psychiatrist, psychoanalyst.

I trust her.

"And now you are back in the world, where a lot of different things are happening to you in every sphere of life, from what you've told me. And now, like everybody else, you have to try to find a way to reckon with these things."

I'm nodding as she says this.

"At least now, we hope, you can. Without the other."

"Yes," I say to her. "Maybe. It's at least a possibility now." I hear myself speaking slowly, taking it in as I express it. But didn't I already know this? Yes—but no one had said it to me before, and I have never said it out loud.

"Are you sure you don't want the name of someone?"

"Yes, I really am."

"I do understand that," says Dr. Prewitt. "*And* respect that. Anyway, the only method a good therapist works with is by pointing out things, by clues that you yourself give him or her, which you then recognize within yourself as true. The patient always does the major part of the work. The patient always has an inner teacher or therapist who is working right along with the outer one. And my own feeling is, sometimes, for some people, the outer therapist may not be completely necessary. In your case, for example, having had so many bad experiences . . . But perhaps not; it depends upon what *you* think and feel and need. But I do know that even a fairly troubled person, if she or he *truly wants* to solve a problem, truly, truly wants to, is truly and heartily tired of being unhappy and suffering, then sometimes that genuine wanting is enough to help awaken that capacity for self-awareness."

"But wouldn't it be easy to hide things from yourself that way?"

"Certainly," says Dr. Prewitt. "And that's why many people prefer to go the route of a good therapist. If one can be found; there are many who, as you know, are not so good. But still, I have seen amazing work done on patients by themselves alone. They just reached a point where they were entirely ready to be transformed."

"Transformed into what?"

"Their best and real selves."

"But how did they know what their best and real selves were?"

"They didn't," says Dr. Prewitt. She half smiles at me. "At least when they started. They just had the certainty that somewhere those best and real selves were out there, or perhaps, more accurately, in there waiting to come out."

I am silent, taking this all in. It blends with all the thoughts I've been having, about choice and nonchoice, about my mother, about being a victim or not being one, about why she doesn't write and why I'm not writing. Like bits of colored glass in a kaleidoscope at the moment when you turn the knob; I feel the pieces tumbling and moving. Will they make a pattern?

Wouldn't it be *boring* if you know your best and real self?

"My own feeling," says Dr. Prewitt, "and it's one many of my colleagues would disagree with, as they disagree with me on vitamin therapy, is that, as I said before, each of us has our own inner teacher or therapist, who, when we are truly ready, can lead us to that best self."

I suppose that the best and real self she is talking about is the one in the very, very center of all the circles.

As I'm getting ready to leave, she asks me, "Elizabeth, the change from being schizophrenic to being what you are now, it's a big one, isn't it?"

"Oh, yes!" I really like her; she's so totally unlike any other shrink I've met. Her hair, which is shoulder length, is always a little messy. She wears regular old professional-woman-type clothes, suits and silk shirts and high-heeled pumps; but she always jazzes them up with some big clunky piece of ethnic jewelry, like today a necklace of big black beads interspersed with little flat pieces of what looks like carved bone. I love the way she always says, "It's my feeling that . . ." instead of just making flat statements.

"That distance you traveled," she says, "from schizophrenia to where you are now, a young woman who is perhaps still scared but no longer hunched over in abject fear, who is well-dressed, quite attractive and self-assured (though I am sure you don't yet realize that you project yourself in such a manner), who had the initiative to seek help about something that troubled her, who is beginning to discover a lively and responsive sexuality so strong it worries her considerably, . . ." and here she smiles. "Well, I truly believe, from what most of my patients tell me, that the journey you have already made is the longest a person can make in her entire life. And you have made it, Elizabeth."

At a newsstand in Grand Central Station, I pick up a copy of the *Village Voice*. I intend to look at the Help Wanted ads and the Apartment for Rent ads; but once I get on the train a dreaminess overtakes me, and I ride with my face pressed to the glass, looking out into the dark at the shimmering river and the lights, reflecting in it. Dr. Prewitt's words keep rising up in me, the pieces of the kaleidoscope move and tumble. They are indeed forming patterns, but I keep turning the knob and they change and change again.

Possibility. Possibility.

But when I get back to Chilton, my mother is waiting with bad news. Mrs. Whittaker called. Tabby tried to kill herself again, but she failed: She is still alive.

No, Tabby, you succeeded: You're alive.

Right after dinner, I sit down and write the Whittakers. My letter isn't perfect, but the second it's finished I fold it, slide it into an envelope, address it, walk to the corner mailbox under the cold, glittering night sky, and drop it in.

Walking back to my mother's house, I begin composing the next letter, the one I will write Tab. And I begin thinking, again, about the ads in the *Village Voice*.

When I get in, Katherine says, "I'm really proud of you, Elizabeth, the way you've taken this news. I was so afraid that it would upset you or . . . set you back."

I want Tab to make it.

I want to make it.

Eleven

Gina

FRIDAY, two weeks later. After meeting my father at Dr. Phipps's and escorting him home a second time, I again leave his apartment on East Forty-seventh Street as soon as I can. This gives me two hours to kill till seven o'clock when I will meet Hal Gillette at a Japanese restaurant downtown. It's already dark when I leave my father's apartment at five and bitterly cold, too cold to walk very far. I stop in a coffee shop called the Flame-Kist about two blocks from my father's. I've been here before. It is called the Flame-Kist because an open grill, with wide bars and glowing orange coals underneath and open flames, is placed along the bank of windows. From the street you can see waving orange flames and the greasy, white-aproned cook spearing steaks and hamburgers. Those hamburgers are just as tasteless as in any mediocre New York coffee shop, despite their authentic-looking black stripes from the grill. My father took me here to eat once, and he made a big deal about the flames and the hamburgers.

"Not bad, hunh? Just-not-bad-at-all!" he said enthusiastically, chomping down on his.

I was sure the only reason he had taken me there was that he was short on cash, a frequent occurrence with my father. Why did he have to do this number about how great the burgers were; why not just admit that they were mediocre, or else not say anything? Did he think I couldn't judge for myself? Did he think I couldn't *taste?* Did he think I wouldn't spend a couple of hours with him if he couldn't afford to take me somewhere good? Or maybe—just maybe—he had truly psyched himself into believing the hamburgers at the Flame-Kist were good, since after all it was only a couple of blocks from him and he probably ate there often.

"You can't sit at the tables without a four-dollar minimum per person after six," says the Flame-Kist waitress to me. She's fortyish and is wearing a red pinafore with the word "Flame-Kist" embroidered in wavy letters that are supposed to look like flames on the left side. She has gigantic breasts that jut out against the pinafore. The rest of her is very skinny, not model-skinny, but unhealthy-skinny.

"It's only ten after five," I say. I'm in a booth, with a fifty-cent cup of coffee. I'm the only customer in the restaurant.

"Look, I'm just tellin' ya," she says, one hand on her hip.

"Would you like me to move to the counter?" I ask her politely.

"Suit y'self." She shrugs and moves off.

My father does have that quality, of being able to psych himself into things. I don't know if he does it consciously. Like with using "groovy"; he probably knows it's outdated but he uses it anyway, and since he does, it's cool. He *makes* it cool. When he moved from Chilton to the apartment I just left him at, at the Belle

Epoch, the first time I came up he said, "So how do you like my little pied-à-terre here, Lizzie-baby?"

I looked around at the scratchy aqua carpet, the grayish-white walls which were textured with this bumpy stucco-y stuff, the low grayish-white ceiling, the one bank of windows looking into the brick side of another building about a foot away, curtained in scratchy aqua. The couch that came with the apartment was fake leather, in olive green, with a chair that matched it and a coffee table.

The apartment was clean; the walls weren't cracked except for one corner in the ceiling; the paint wasn't peeling; and I'd only seen a couple of roaches, unusually few for New York. But it struck me as what I picture as the interior of cheap motel rooms, the X-rated kind with dirty movies on big video screens. It was very quiet. Not a peaceful quiet, but a mausoleum, embalmed quiet. My father's typewriter, on its gray metal table in a corner, his old office chair, both of which had always been kept in his upstairs office back in Chilton, his magazines and books and papers, all looked impermanent and fragile and temporary, as if the wind had somehow blown them in and tomorrow could blow them away again; except you couldn't imagine anything alive and natural and forceful as wind coming into the apartment.

That is how I had always seen my father, too: forceful, alive like a natural force, *super*alive, more alive than other people. So how had he wound up at the Belle Epoch, with its low ceilings and stucco-y walls? I could have pictured him more easily sleeping on a Central Park bench with newspapers wrapped around him, *or* striding confidently through the Plaza lobby down to a waiting limousine. Something extreme, with him loudly proclaiming its virtues. The freedom and fresh air of the park bench: the elegance and history of the Plaza; the interesting, fascinating captivating people you could meet, *only* at . . . wherever he was. Nothing in between seemed right for my father. Certainly not this apartment, a few stops above shabby but a lot of stops below elegant or homey.

"So what do you think, Lizzie-baby?"

I said, cautiously, "Well, it seems a little sterile to me."

"Sterile! Whaddya mean, sterile? This place is not sterile, whaddya talking about?" He was furious. It reminded me of the time when I was nine and my brother, who had just turned eighteen, called my father, in response to what I cannot remember, bourgeois, and my father bellowed, "OUT! OUT OF THE HOUSE, STEPH! NO ONE CALLS ME BOURGEOIS IN MY OWN HOUSE! OUT!" And Steph packed a bag and left and wound up joining the army and that was that.

It also reminded me of the Left Bank fight, which was earlier; Steph was still around then. The gist of it was, my father wanted us to move from Chilton to the Left Bank in Paris, France—all of us, the whole family. He screamed at my mother, "You're choking me! Chilton is choking me!" Doing my hated math homework on the long oak table in the dining room, I knew exactly what he meant because I felt the same way as far as Chilton was concerned. Though tensed up by the fight, and sorry for my mother, I was terribly excited about the idea of the family going to live in France, in Paris. I would learn to speak French. I would be the exotic, foreign, mysterious new girl at my French school, popular, sought-after, free of the Mary Theresa Buglianos calling me "four-eyes" and "dirty Jew."

Now I know moving to Paris was just another one of my father's ideas that we had no money for. Even then my mother was working at Rahleigh, supporting all of us, while my father dreamed the dreams he believed, wrongly and in anger, my mother was keeping from coming true.

"No," I said to my father when he took me to Flame-Kist, after swallowing the bit of dry, grayed, charred meat in my mouth. "No, it's not bad at all, Walter."

At five minutes to six o'clock I leave the Flame-Kist, leaving the waitress who has been evil-eyeing me a dollar tip. I shouldn't leave her anything since she was so nasty, but I want to prove her wrong about me.

I take the bus downtown, squinting my eyes out the window to make the lights in the passing buildings and shop windows blur together like an impressionist painting. The air is moist and warm in the bus except when the door opens and lets in another blast of cold air as someone gets in or out. It smells of damp wool and wet leather boots, and the floor is damp and puddled with muddy crumbs of melting ice. Across the aisle from me is a black lady in a blue knit hat with a shopping bag and a brown purse and rubbers on her shoes, wearing a brown coat. Farther down is a boy of maybe eighteen, with dark, floppy hair and intense dark eyes, not looking at anything in particular but drawn into himself, deep in thought, hunched down, half scowling. He's carrying an artist's portfolio. From Forty-second Street to Twenty-third, I live my life with this young man, who has extravagantly long eyelashes; we share an apartment, we shop together on weekends, we bring home string bags laden with fresh vegetables and cheeses, long French breads sticking out at the top. I pose for him, nude, lying on my side. . . . Do I go out and work while he stays at home and paints, or does he go out while I stay home and write? I settle it: We both work at home. I put us in bed, a platform bed he's built, with drawers underneath. We laugh, we know what each other's thinking, then he's moving over me; the way his hair would hang into my face, the way he would kiss me on the lips . . . Hidden under layers of clothing, my nipples get hard. Even after he gets off the bus I'm still hot and bothered, a phrase that has had new meaning to me since having that wonderful sex with Jonathan Tuesday night. (I can't resist him much longer, I know, and there's really no reason why I should; except I don't like him and then it'll be back in the quicksand again, though since that first climax with Jon I have been mentally in the quicksand anyway.)

And all the time I am observing these people and having these thoughts, the camera is going click, click, click.

Yet every person on this bus has their own story, surely very different from what the camera sees. Probably some of them even make up stories about the people they see, like I do. I can't even begin to guess their stories accurately any more than I can guess the Flame-Kist waitress's life, any more than someone could guess mine. Who could imagine, from looking at me, that I've just picked my father up after his second shock treatment?

When the black lady gets off the bus she hands me a pamphlet and says, "God bless you, chile." The pamphlet's title is, "Are You SURE . . . About the World Hereafter?"

I answer to myself, "No, I'm not even sure about this one." I open the pamphlet and skim it. It's dotted with capitalized words: SIN, SALVATION, THE LORD, PERSONAL SAVIOR.

For some reason I think about Tabby. I can easily imagine us, us as we were a year or two back, going into a whole routine over this. "Hey, I'm not SURE, about anything, are you, Lizzie-Liz?"

I'd say, "Well, SURE I'm SURE!"

Given the most minimal cause, Tabby and I used to be able to laugh ourselves silly.

"Stop-stop-stop you're making my mascara run!"

We often incited each other in laughter to the point where tears came to our eyes.

Once, at a little restaurant in Provincetown, someone came over to the table and said, "Julie . . . Miss Christie. . . ." He was a middle-aged guy; he'd left a slightly dumpy but pleasant enough woman at his table.

"Yes?" said Tabby.

"Would it be an imposition if I asked for your autograph?"

"Not at all," said Tabby graciously. On a napkin, she, Tabitha Whittaker, signed *Julie Christie*.

"Thank you, thank you very much, I truly appreciate this," said the man, smiling broadly and obsequiously. "I loved your performance in *Shampoo*. Well, I don't want to bother you anymore; thank you again so much."

"It's nothing," said Tabby. "Thank *you.*"

I could scarcely control myself; but when he left the table, I was astonished to see that Tabby wasn't laughing. She looked serious, almost grave.

"What's wrong?" I asked her.

"Nothing."

"I can't believe you did that."

"Oh, Elizabeth," she said, very sadly. "It's so pitifully easy to make people ecstatically happy sometimes."

She would have understood why I tipped the waitress a buck, why I am on my way to see Hal Gillette even though since I went to bed with Jonathan doing so again is all that's been on my mind: well, not all, but kind of constantly *there,* at a low hot simmer.

Tabby got expelled from Lakeland for getting caught in bed with Paul Viguerie. Paul got only two weeks' suspension. *Ms.* magazine should write an exposé.

Later, when I remember this evening, the bus ride and my thoughts on it are the last things I clearly recall because the poetry reading later overshadowed everything else. I know that I got to the Japanese restaurant; it was up a flight of stairs, above a store that sold imported Indian clothes like tiered gauze skirts. I remember the restaurant was dark, and that Hal was waiting for me, and that we shared an order of tempura to start. But I cannot remember one word I said to Hal, or he to me, over dinner, probably because I was doing my "unh-hunh, unh-hunh, *really,* isn't that interesting," number, of seeming to listen raptly, actually not listening at all.

In fact, later it seems to me that God (though I'm not even sure I believe in Him or Her) worked out the whole thing, first Hal's talking to me in the museum, and later our sleeping together, expressly to get me to Gina's reading that night. It does seem a bit circuitous for God to have gone through all that when you think that I could have simply learned about the poetry reading just by reading the announcement in the *Village Voice* when I was looking at ads for apartments. But in any case I got there, through Hal, and maybe through God.

Trying to write about Gina Cristalle Morgenthau's reading makes me realize how much easier it is to describe bad events than good ones.

If I tell you that she was in her mid-thirties, was not tall but seemed tall, was not beautiful but seemed beautiful, and that her poetry was funny and wicked and precise and sad and wise, with each word chosen to flow into the next with a breathtaking and sensual exactness of meaning and sound and rhythm and contrast—if I tell you all that, it still leaves out her *presence*. It leaves out the way I felt in that presence, which was as if I was suddenly bathed in warm light, soft, peachy-golden, illuminating and distinct, bright but gentle, not harsh. It was as if the rest of my life was *out there*, a dark, a cold desert spreading out boundlessly, shifting sands; but within that room, with Gina Cristalle Morgenthau reading, I was safe, I was by a campfire in a walled green, tropical oasis garden. I was absorbed, rapt, utterly removed from that life of darkness that was my life. I was as lost to myself as when seeing a totally absorbing movie, or reading a fine book, or, sometimes, writing my own poems. The camera was *not* on, not clicking.

You could say that I glimpsed a possibility, listening to her, or that she articulated my secrets, then took them one step further.

I know everybody has now heard of Gina, but she was then much less well known and she was certainly unknown to me. There were about fifty people at the reading, and at the back of the room was a large table with several of her books for sale. Immediately after the reading people flocked to her, and to the book table; but I sat in my folding chair literally unable to move, so strong was her spell on me.

"Elizabeth? D'you like it?"

When I turned to look at Hal, for a second I truly did not know who he was. Not his name, not his relationship to me. I opened my mouth and shut it. The regular, ordinary world came back then, but I knew it was changed. Or I was.

I nodded yes to Hal.

"You ready to go?"

I shook my head.

"You all right?"

"Oh, yes, fine," I said, finding words but feeling them foreign and clumsy in my mouth. "I just, if you don't mind, I want to buy some of her books and maybe have her sign them for me," which I could see other people were doing.

"Well, fine, I'll just stretch my legs and check this place out—It's some kind of alternative arts school or something—and maybe I'll get a breath of fresh air. Sure you don't want to come? Looks like she'll be there for a while, you can come back in a few minutes."

"I'll wait."

After I had bought, using a week's worth of lunch money, *Colored Inks, Letters from the Fruit Market, The Difference Between Doors and Windows,* and *Unfurling for Flight,* I stood in line to talk to her and have her sign my books. I was at the end of the line, which was how I wanted it. I didn't know what I was going to say to her; I just knew I didn't want someone behind me listening, impatiently waiting his turn.

By the time I reached Gina, she looked a little tired, but she took the books from my hand as she gazed up at me, quickly scanning my face.

"Are these for you?" she asked. As she looked up it occurred to me that we looked a bit alike: semitic features; same shade of brown hair, though hers was fuller and longer; same color eyes, though hers were bluer and completely without cloudiness.

I nodded.

"What I mean is," she said kindly, "do you want them inscribed to you?"

Again, still speechless, I nodded.

Laughter unlaughed rippled the edges of her mouth.

She raised her eyebrows and looked right, *right* at me. "In that case," she said gently, "you'd better give me your name."

"Oh! Elizabeth Stein."

"The way it sounds?"

"Yes."

She looked down. She opened *Letters from the Fruit Market* and pressed back the cover, uncapped her pen and held it above the page.

"Wait!" I said.

She looked up at me again, expectant, face open and ready to listen. In the open, energetic quality of her face, in the way she seemed almost lit up, there was something distantly familiar to me. But I wasn't sure what it was or what I wanted to say.

"Thank you," I began, and stopped. To put into words what I had felt when she was reading seemed cumbersome, artificial. Perhaps impossible. Still, she waited. "Hearing you read was important for me, Ms. Morgenthau. . . ."

"Gina."

"Gina. Some of what you read went through me. 'Duration's from within or not at all,' in that poem about wondering whether to telephone someone. . . ."

She nodded, her gaze bright upon me.

"Or that one about the unripe avocados ripening. The one with the line 'scarves of very glossy leaves,' about being bitter but patient with your own bitterness so you could learn to be wise and be kind of returned to whatever innocence you might have once had before you became bitter and . . ." I trailed off, but she nodded again. "Well," I said, "I don't want to be making assumptions about what you meant, but . . ."

"But that is what I meant," she said. "And even if I hadn't, a poem has a life of its own, and how a reader responds to that life has meaning, even, maybe especially, if that response isn't what the poet originally intended. So, don't feel awkward."

"But your poems are so articulate, and for me to try to paraphrase them or tell you what they meant to me or how they make me feel . . ."

"I work to get my poems that way," she said, amused. "I'm not that way in casual conversation. If you liked my work so much you feel inarticulate about expressing it, that's a great compliment to me. Which I thank you for."

I gazed down at her.

"Elizabeth," she said. "Would you like to sit down?"

I nodded and fell into a chair next to her.

She pushed some wavy dark brown hair off her forehead.

"Elizabeth," she repeated. She narrowed her eyes, looking at me intensely. "Do you mind my asking you a personal question?"

"No."

"How old are you?"

"How old would you guess?"

"I would guess," she said slowly, "that you are younger than you look. Am I right?"

I nodded.

"Eighteen, nineteen?"

"Seventeen."

"It's unusual for people your age to come to my readings," she said. "I'm glad you were here."

We looked at each other. I still sensed that odd, lit-up energy crackling from her. Of course! What was familiar to me was that this was what I felt all those years ago from the black jazz musician.

And then I got: This is it. This is what all that self-awareness, best- and real-self stuff is about. Here is a person living a life of self-understanding. It's not abstract, not dull. Neither, from her poems—and from those notes I can still remember, trickling down out of that silver flute in the dark night—is it painless. But what it is, is doing the thing that makes you completely, fully alive, alive behind words—that's why the words feel awkward to me now, that's why I reached for that tall, handsome black man all those years ago—doing the only thing that matters for you no matter what the consequences are.

And for me, I know very well that thing is writing.

And if my mother wanted to do it like this, she would.

I rocked under the impact of all this.

Gina, meanwhile, got up, poured herself a glass of water from a pitcher on the podium, offered me one—I shook my head—sat back down. She took a sip.

"And do you write?" she asked me.

I nodded.

"Poetry?"

"And a journal. Off and on." I pause. "But I want to do novels."

"You're not doing them yet?" I shook my head. "Then you must start right away." She was quite serious. "A writer writes. It's that simple. A lot of people say, 'I've always wanted to write,' and I truly believe it's a genuine enough impulse, given how many extraordinary things happen to most people. But real writers, and I don't mean published or unpublished, I mean people with the true urge that will carry them through all the obstacles that come up to block them, that will even help them make those obstacles part of the work, real writers say, 'I've always written.' And they keep on writing."

"Well, I have written always, just not novels." Then

I thought back. "At least, not in years. I started a couple when I was in grade school."

"Then you must start again. Do it."

"I will, I will!" She and I were speaking lightly, but both of us knew we were serious.

She took a couple of sips of water, looking away from me as she did so. Then, returning that bright, strange gaze to me, she said, "Several of the poems I read tonight I wrote when I was only a little older than you, nineteen, twenty or so. Most of *Colored Inks* is from that period.

"It's a hard period, not young and not adult. I wrote a lot then. And I sometimes feel I could write forever drawing on just what happened and what I was feeling during those years. A very difficult time, but a very fertile time for a writer."

Again I nodded.

"That's one thing about difficult periods, they make for excellent writing. One is driven to it. Now that I am happy, I do much less poetry. Some prose, but not much poetry."

"*Are* you happy?" I asked her. I have never heard someone say this, flat out, without qualifications, *I am happy.* It's something people put in the future. If only I had this. After I have that.

She nodded. "Yes, I am. Not that there are not difficulties, but I have an active spiritual life; my work is going well; I make enough money; and I have the great good fortune to have married extremely well, I mean well in my own terms. Don't look so disappointed! Not all marriages diminish people."

"But you seem so complete!"

She smiles. "Elizabeth," she says. "The very best marriages, the good ones, and there aren't too many of them around, are between two people who *are* relatively complete. Now, I think you have to be alone a lot to *get* complete, at least I did, to learn enough about yourself so you can love someone else well and *be* loved well. If you can remember that, perhaps you can avoid some disasters. Probably not, though; God knows I didn't. You'll need the disasters for your work, anyway."

"I've had them."

"Yes," she said, a little sadly, "somehow I thought you might have."

She looked at me, giving me the option of going further.

I said, "I don't know why I'm telling you this, but my father is having shock treatments; I pick him up afterwards. My parents are getting divorced. My mother depends on me too much and makes me feel guilty most of the time. I have two boyfriends, I'm not crazy about either of them. One of them is really, really good in bed. I'm afraid my best friend is going to kill herself, and I don't know if there's anything I can do to stop it. I go to a progressive school now and I hate it, but it's the only place that would take me in because last summer I was in two mental hospitals."

"Another personal question," she said. "Suicide attempt get you in there?"

I nodded.

"I don't know why I'm doing this either," she said, "but here goes." Gina Cristalle Morgenthau was wearing jeans and a loose, full, plum-colored velour pullover with a cowl neck and ribbed waist and cuffs and padded shoulders and full drapey sleeves. Slowly she pushed her left sleeve up past her black-banded watch, all the way to her elbow.

Scars lined her wrist, scars a pale white—mine are still red—ancient, barely visible pale white lines threading her inner forearm. I looked from her scarred arm to her face. Our eyes met.

And then I reached out and put my arms around her, as I did all those years ago in the sculpture garden. Celebration, admiration, something fine beyond words.

And yet, different. Then, I hadn't had words; now, I had them but knew their limits. Then, I was a child, reaching toward a grown man, a magic man who picked me up, hard, firm, black, tall. Now, I was a woman, hugging a woman, hugging someone, something, that was like me: soft, white, rounded, same size, same height. Both of our feet were on the ground, we were celebrating the picking up of ourselves, by ourselves, our survival, our writing—hers already begun, mine still to be, yet also, in its way, already begun.

Different and identical, full circle.

Later, after she had signed my books, she said, in answer to my unasked question, "Look, Elizabeth, I'm not going to give you my phone number because it's difficult for me to be involved with people on a casual level and I sort of have to save myself, protect myself, for my work. It's not that I wouldn't help you if I could; I just know this is the best way I can. Do you understand?"

Oddly, I did. Each of the twenty or twenty-five people ahead of me on the line tonight had told Gina something about themselves, or wanted something from her, because something in them was awoken by or spoken to in her poetry. Quickly I realized that that quality about Gina and her work which permits "unfurling for flight," costs her something, at least when she shares it publicly. Though it also nourishes her in some way—and in that realization I felt I had learned something essential about poetry, about life, about the rings and circles. About, again as she put it, "the difference between doors and windows." Windows you can see out of, catch glimpses, but doors you go *through*, you can actually enter and exit from. Gina had given me a window and showed me a door I had sensed was there all along. It was the same door, in a way, Dr. Prewitt had alluded to, but Gina had actually shown it to me. Yet it was still up to me to unlock it, turn the handle, push it open, and walk to the other side.

"But," Gina said, "you know, I also believe in the chance meeting, the fortuitous encounter, maybe even the miraculous one, where it's not whom you meet so much as who you are, something in you that's all ripe and ready and somehow gets set off. It's happened to me a couple of times, and I think this may be one, some small chance meeting that has changed or touched me, an epiphany."

"This has been that for me," I said, though I didn't then know the meaning of the word epiphany.

She took my hand and looked me in the eye one more time: the last time. Her eyes were startlingly blue and clear. "Hold on, Elizabeth. Endure, take risks, put it all in your work, and work hard." She squeezed my hand. "Don't confuse being fed on, or feeding on someone, with love, or try not to. Mostly, you have to work hard. You have to persist, with diligence and honesty and humility and. . ." with her other hand she reached up and touched my face, tapping my cheek very lightly, "a certain amount of impertinence."

Hal Gillette is waiting for me outside the door. "I peered in, but you were deep in conversation and I didn't want to interrupt you."

"Thanks," I say, and as I look at Hal I feel that for the first time I am looking at him from inside myself.

"You're a nice guy, Hal," I tell him. "You really are. I'm sorry to tell you this, but I have been extremely dishonest with you." I tell him my real age, occupation, a little history.

Hal is thunderstruck. On the way out I pick up an Alternative University schedule. Hal keeps saying, "I just can't believe it, you're the same age as my kids! I can't believe it! As my seniors!"

After I talk him into taking the subway home and letting me get to Grand Central on my own, I go into the little India Imports place. Though it's now nearly eleven, it's still open. I spend most of my money on a shirt. As I do so, I'm aware that it's really Katherine's money; but, first of all, I know that no matter what she says sometimes, she would truly celebrate with me what I am celebrating by this purchase. And, number two, I know now that I'm not far away from earning my own money. I'm going to talk to that girl at Barnes & Noble on Monday. I'm going to make a lot of changes. But in some ways they aren't changes, in some ways they're a return.

The shirt has big built-up shoulders and this wonderful inset triangular collar that drapes in the middle but buttons up high on the neck, sort of cossacky.

The shirt is a bright, solid, true red.

It's not till I'm going home on the train that I open my books to see what Gina has written. In three, she's just signed her name and "for Elizabeth," but in the fourth, *Unfurling for Flight,* she's written:

> For Elizabeth, unfurling.
> With hope and confidence in the flight,
> Gina (who looks like you)

It's the word "confidence," underlined, that gets me.

The Hudson, dark and cold, flows by the warm, lit, dirty train, almost empty at this hour. I look out at it for a while.

Then I open my purse and fish around and I find it: the small spiral-bound notebook I always carry. I have carried one with me for years. Tabby used to kid me about it; but I had a line I had picked up somewhere, I think it was Oscar Wilde who said it when asked why he always carried his diary: "But one must always have something sensational to read on the train, my dear!"

This one is completely blank; it has never been used, like the previous one, the one that had only my name and address in it but saved my life anyway. I never got that one back. This one was the first thing I purchased when I got out of the hospitals and was free to go into stores again.

On the first page I write:

Jay's wake (not a wake).
Katherine. Oranges. Driving with D. Fiori. Ice.
Tabby. Hitchhiking to Stockbridge.
Walter. Kris. Picking him up at Phipps's ofc.

The train shakes and jerks, adding jagged peaks and valleys to my handwriting. I sit there and look at this list for a while, in fine-line black felt tip, on the pale-blue college-ruled lines, in the spiral notebook. Then I look out the window again into the dark. And I know my life is for this.

If there is meaning to what has happened to me this year, I will find it as I write about it.

And if there is not meaning to what has happened to me this year, I will still find it as I write about it.

I pick up the notebook again and I turn to the next page. On it I write: *I have the mother everyone wants.*

At home, my mother is still up, reading in the living room by the fire in a long blue caftan. I feel a surge of happiness, seeing that she has made a fire for herself, just herself, to enjoy privately, without me or Walter or Steph being there. She deserves it.

Maybe, after I leave, she will learn to do lots of things for her own enjoyment.

Maybe she will either quit Rahleigh and Byrd or find a way to do the things she seems to like—discovering authors like Edmund Weller, and working with him and Tania Shavelson and Renaldo Sant'Angelo and the rest, even Cam Peckinpaker (well, maybe she'll learn to muzzle Cam some)—and not do the things she dislikes: office politics, infighting with Phil Heindorf.

Maybe, whether she quits at Rahleigh or not, she will write her novel.

But maybe not.

Blue looks good on her, any shade of blue. She is thrilled to see me. For once this doesn't annoy me or make me feel guilty.

"Why, honey, what a surprise! I thought you were going to a poetry reading and then staying over with one of your friends!"

"I went to the poetry reading, but then I decided to come home."

"Was it good?"

"Yes, wonderful."

"Want something to eat?"

"In a minute, first I—"

"What's in the bag?"

"Oh, Katherine, I bought this beautiful shirt, it's—"

"Oh, honey!" she says. "I'm glad, I'm so glad! I'm

so glad you bought something for yourself!'' And indeed she does look exultant.

And suddenly I realize this is because, other than books, this is the only thing I've bought for myself since getting out of the hospital. What she feels may be *Maybe my daughter will have a future.*

What she doesn't, can't know, is that all this time, even when *I* didn't know it, I was making one.

And, in a way, perhaps the feeling of seeing her beside the fire had the same meaning to me.

''It's red,'' I tell her. ''It's a great, big, bright, bright red.''

''Oh, red's always looked good on you.''

''I've been thinking since I came in how good blue looks on *you.*''

''Want to try your new shirt on for me after you get out of your coat and have a bite to eat?'' She's still beaming; I can't recall when I have seen her look so happy.

''In a minute, in a minute. I have to look something up first.'' I cross the living room to the dictionary on its stand.

''What?'' asks my mother, meaning, what word.

''*Epiphany,*'' I say. ''I think I just had one.''